CN00767779

BOUNTY HUNTER

BAD BOYS IN BIG TROUBLE 5

FIONA ROARKE

BOUNTY HUNTER
Copyright © 2016 Fiona Roarke

ALL RIGHTS RESERVED. No part of this book may be reproduced in any form or by any electronic or mechanical means, including photocopying, recording, or information storage and retrieval systems—except in the case of brief quotations embodied in critical articles or reviews—without permission in writing from the author.

This book is a work of fiction. The characters, organizations, events, and places portrayed in this book are products of the author's imagination and are either fictitious or are used fictitiously. Any similarity to a real person, living or dead is purely coincidental and not intended by the author.

Nickel Road Publishing
ISBN: 978-1-944312-10-7

Published in the United States of America

Want to know when Fiona's next book will be available?
Sign up for her Newsletter: http://eepurl.com/bONukX

DEDICATION

*For my writing friends who keep me grounded, sane
and moving in the right direction.*

Books by Fiona Roarke

Dalton Langston has a sixth sense when it comes to tracking his quarry. He has a talent for getting in his prey's mind. Now, the only thing he's interested in hunting is some rest and relaxation in Las Vegas. The last thing he wants is to get dragged into chasing after some runaway rich girl.

Lina Dragovic has eluded everyone her parents have sent after her in their efforts to force her into an arranged marriage. She's served her time as the Dragovic crime family's cloistered daughter. Now all she wants is her freedom. What better place to hide than Sin City, where the bright lights offer the deepest shadows?

But there's no outrunning the dangerously sexy bounty hunter...especially when getting caught by him is so tempting. And so deliciously rewarding.

Falling in love was never part of the plan.

Bounty Hunter, Bad Boys in Big Trouble 5
Nothing's sexier than a good man gone bad boy.

PROLOGUE

"Nikolina, for heaven's sake, stand up straight," her mother ordered in a terse tone. "You're going to be a bride to one of the richest families from the homeland. Pretend like you are happy for five seconds."

Nikolina Dragovic, known as Lina to everyone in her world with the exception of her old-fashioned parents, stared at her reflection in the angled three-panel mirror at the most exclusive bridal boutique in Ironwood, Arizona.

Perhaps she should be happy, but she was not. She straightened her mouth from a frown to a neutral expression. She was in no mood to smile. Simply *not* frowning outright was the best she could manage.

The elaborate and insanely expensive wedding gown felt heavy and uncomfortable, like equal parts shroud and falsehood, dragging her deeper into despair. She did not want to be here. Her mother, however, didn't care about her feelings in this matter.

Lina straightened and felt a pinch near her shoulder blades. Damn, this dress was heavy. There must be thirty pounds of pearls sewn into the fabric. Given that this was a custom creation priced in the high five figures, that was likely typical for such decadence.

Heavy and elaborate equaled stylish and classy in Martina Dragovic's mind. If Lina didn't concentrate on keeping her body tilted slightly forward as she walked to balance the weight, any wind, stiff or not, would knock her backwards onto her ass and a hoist might be required to get her upright again.

The ten-foot train—that her mother insisted made her look like royalty—felt more like an anchor she'd have to drag down the aisle to her ultimate fate.

Marriage.

But not just any marriage.

Lina's marriage had been arranged. An unusual custom for this day and age, but her family had been participating in such practices for a long time. They'd brought the arranged marriage custom with them to the United States two generations ago from Kzeratia. She was destined to marry into a rich family from the country her grandparents had left decades ago in search of what they called a better life.

Unlike many coming to this country, her grandparents had been wealthy. They brought their riches to their new home and set about earning even more money at a faster rate.

They had succeeded admirably. Each member of her extended family had more than they could possibly spend in ten lifetimes, but her parents always wanted more.

As the only child and daughter of Martina and Ivan Dragovic, she'd grown up knowing she had a specific duty to perform for her parents. Had she been a son, she would have been obligated to helm the family business. A daughter's duty was to marry someone her parents selected, knowing he would also take on the responsibility for the business.

Unlike her mother and grandmothers, Lina wouldn't be obligated to remain in a loveless marriage for the rest of her life. A recent scandal had changed everything. She had an out. She'd bargained hard for it. She intended to take advantage of her escape clause at the first opportunity.

She had never met her bridegroom. Even with the technology available to change that, her parents felt *that* information was inconsequential to the process.

It didn't matter what he looked like or sounded like or anything so superfluous as knowledge of his education or interests. He had a good family name back in the homeland and, most importantly, lots of money. His family was less showy about their riches than hers. However, both families agreed on one thing quite ardently. Inherited wealth should be preserved for the family line at all costs. Merging families to maintain wealth was the standard in the circles Lina's family moved in, and arranged marriages to virtual strangers for profit had remained a tradition for centuries.

Lina would discover all she needed to know about her bridegroom when he arrived in the States after they'd married by proxy.

Apparently, her mysterious bridegroom faced the same parental restrictions she did when it came to an online presence—not a big surprise, since he was bound for the same antiquated marriage arrangement she was—because a quick look online when she last visited the local library had yielded nothing in the way of a single photograph of her intended or his uber-rich family. What he looked like would remain a secret until he arrived in Arizona.

Her parents felt they knew best, just like their parents had known best for them. That philosophy had been used for quite a few generations to help create the family wealth they now enjoyed.

Arranged marriages were the norm in her family; happiness wasn't. From Lina's perspective, both sets of grandparents had been miserable.

Her parents were equally unhappy, but were united in their zeal not only to increase their wealth through conventional business means, but also to see *her* marriage arranged as theirs had been, for financial goals. So while they had the happiest marriage in her family, it was most assuredly not based on love. Greed ruled their hearts.

Lina didn't care about money the way her parents did. It was necessary, of course, but she didn't have the same obsessive drive to hoard money like the rest of her relatives. She'd love to live a much simpler life. She'd never shared her feelings on that subject with her parents. Her thoughts of running away to live free, poor and alone were reserved for daydreams. She didn't even put her foolish notions down on paper for fear she'd be found out.

A recent scandal in her parents' circle of wealthy friends involving a girl her age had changed everything in Lina's life for the better. Before, the arranged marriage had loomed like a punishment she had to endure because that's the way it had always been. But now, the fear of scandal worked in her favor. The loathsome arranged marriage became a vehicle for her freedom.

When she initiated a conversation to discuss the coming wedding plans, Lina referenced the scandalous behavior that had made such recent headlines. Then she added her own wedding stipulations. Her parents were shocked and livid, but she held firm. They reluctantly agreed to her wishes. However, they also wanted her to try to find common ground with her new husband. They thought perhaps the stranger they wanted her to marry might somehow win her over. She wasn't as convinced, but promised to be open to his charms—if he possessed any.

Lina had long despaired of having the life she wanted, but tried to keep her singular condition and goal in mind: Freedom. Eventually, she'd be awarded her liberty to pursue whatever she wanted, if certain conditions had not been met within the marriage. And she'd gotten it in writing.

First and foremost, she didn't want to settle down in one place. She wanted to see the world. She wanted to explore. She wanted to travel. She didn't really want to get married, not yet. Maybe someday, but certainly not now and not to some stranger from a country she'd never even visited. Her dreams didn't coincide with her family's unending plans to hoard money. Travel was lumped into spending money for pleasure, and not something she should desire.

Lina especially didn't want to marry some man her parents selected based on a prestigious family name and an impressive financial history to match. She wanted to fall in love. She wanted someone who made her laugh, someone who would be loyal only to her, someone who didn't want to stockpile money like her parents.

There were rumors that the groom's family was second only to the Dragovic clan in regards to shady business dealings, both in the States and in Kzeratia, but they were only rumors.

Lina wanted no part of her parents' business or her temporary future in-laws' business either. Her preselected husband would fill that role for her family and his. Like the son her parents had wanted, but couldn't have.

Lina stared at her sad image in the mirror. She hated this whole process and the dress she wore and not being able to make her own choices.

She again tried for a neutral expression, a cool mask that would hide her innermost feelings. If all went as planned, she would eventually have her choices and her freedom. She must hold onto that dream.

"Why do you have to do this, Lina?" Petra Kovac

asked for seemingly the thousandth time. Seated at the foot of the bed in Petra's well-appointed room, Lina crossed her arms loosely, trying to remain relaxed. Petra extracted dresses from her closet, one by one, trying to find the perfect attire for a proxy wedding.

She forced a smile for her best friend. "I told you. Tradition." It was becoming more difficult to spout the family line. But as she'd told herself earlier at the bridal boutique, she must keep her eye on the prize. While the proxy wedding took place tomorrow, her new husband wouldn't arrive for another couple of weeks.

Petra's face was the picture of frustration and unhappiness. "My family came from the old country, too, and I can marry anyone I want, even if he is not from Kzeratia."

Her friend held up another dress as a possibility for the wedding ceremony tomorrow. Lina nodded at the pretty blue print dress and Petra put it next to the pink dress she'd selected earlier as a candidate.

"Your parents are modern and progressive. My parents are old-fashioned, with values from two centuries ago. They like to keep with the customs of our ancestors. They want to see that the old ways are carried forward." *And most of all, they want to protect all that money they've accumulated and add to it.*

Petra's family had emigrated to the United States in search of better prospects, too, but they had a different idea as to what constituted opportunity. One that didn't involve treating marriage like a business transaction and their daughter as currency.

Lina clung to her hard-won hope of eventual freedom. She thanked her lucky stars for the young woman who'd done the unspeakable and eloped with a simple bartender before her own proxy marriage could happen. The parents in that case had been unable to separate their daughter from what had turned out to be a fortune hunter, and their carefully laid plans of an arranged marriage to build prestige and wealth were ruined.

It had created the biggest scandal in their social world in the past hundred years, maybe more. It also provided Lina with the perfect sway over her parents and their marriage plans.

After that disgraceful incident rocked their social sphere, Lina initiated a discussion to talk about her specific situation. Her parents had not been very happy, but Lina told them she thought the elopement had been romantic, even if it didn't turn out as the girl had planned.

Lina's parents suddenly feared she might do the same thing. So they accepted her proposal of a deal that would preserve both of their wishes. To a degree.

Her parents promised that once the dictates of the marriage contract had been fulfilled and her intended, Mislav Zupan, had attained his citizenship, she would be allowed to seek a quiet divorce.

She'd then be free to make a life of her own, based on her specific choices, with a little bit of money to do as she wished.

Two years of marriage for a lifetime of freedom.

Lina had leapt at the chance.

Of course, she might actually fall for Mislav, especially if he had progressive ideas and a yen to travel. It was a long shot and not a gamble she was willing to risk everything on, thus the signed document she'd hidden away in a backpack in her closet.

Her parents were also contractually obligated to pay her a modest reward at the end of her "duty," although she didn't want to count on those funds. She also didn't want money to rule her life as it had her parents' existence. She wanted to make her own way in the world, where the Dragovic name didn't color how people treated her.

She knew her parents believed the promise of money

at the end of her contract would keep Lina in line. If she left the marriage before two years were up, she'd leave with nothing but the clothes on her back and whatever she could save from any allowance her husband offered. If he offered nothing, as her parents had strongly suggested he do, she'd be screwed. Or so her parents thought.

Luckily, she had a plan for that eventuality, thanks to Granny Kerima.

Her father's mother, her favorite grandmother, managed to squirrel away a nice nest egg in the course of her own disagreeable marriage. It turned out that Granny Kerima had a talent for day trading, of all things. Working in secret, she'd increased that nest egg a hundredfold. Half of those earnings were in an ironclad account meant only for Lina on her twenty-fourth birthday, less than three years from now. Her parents couldn't touch it. Only Lina could get the money the day she turned twenty-four or any time after.

It wasn't enough to live on forever, simply a nice little chunk of change to fund a long trip to an exotic place or use to start over with an uncomplicated life. Lina wanted away from the lives her parents and grandparents had led. She had no interest in running an "alleged" criminal empire or even being adjacent to one for the remainder of her life.

Lina suspected Granny Kerima wished *she'd* had that option long ago.

She was very grateful to her granny, but wished she didn't have to wait to collect. If her husband-to-be was an ogre or expected more than an in-name-only marriage, he'd be able to make her life miserable until he became a citizen. Two years bound to a stranger was a long time if he didn't cooperate.

"What do you think Mislav looks like?" Petra asked breaking her troubled reverie.

"Not a clue. His parents are even less accepting of social media than mine and that takes some doing." Not that it mattered. Lina didn't care what he looked like. She was more concerned about what he might demand from her once they were legally husband and wife. Her parents could only protect her so far. Even in their social circles, a mistreated wife often bore the brunt of any blame associated with marital disagreements.

If Mislav agreed to all the terms set forth in the marriage contract, they would have the same official address, but she'd live elsewhere, with her parents most likely, and only report with him for regular meetings to prove to the immigration officials they were a loving couple living a happily married life.

Despite her carefully laid plans, Lina had trouble controlling her misgivings. "Are you still coming to the ceremony tomorrow, Petra?"

"I wouldn't miss it. Maybe the proxy agent will bring a poster-sized picture of your intended and stand it up next to you. You know, like at a funeral with a closed-casket service."

"Morbid." Lina rolled her eyes skyward.

"Realistic," Petra insisted. "Besides, then you could at least get a look at him at your big wedding. Maybe he's a dreamy prince." Petra was forever a romantic.

Lina, on the other hand, was pragmatic in all things. "You have such foolish optimism for what's sure to be a boring ceremony to an ugly, rich frog."

"No. I have a rabid fascination for an antiquated practice still being used in this day and age. This is like a marriage of convenience in a romance novel."

Petra the Romantic strikes again. "I'm not convinced this is going to be a romance in any way, shape or form. But whatever happens, I'm glad you'll be there with me."

"What are friends for?" Petra threw her skinny arms

around Lina's neck and squeezed hard. She returned the hug, fighting back a sudden pang of gratitude.

Lina was so grateful Petra would be in her life as she made her way through the next two years married to either a frog or a prince.

The next day went exactly as Lina expected. The proxy agent was a stodgy looking lawyer in an expensive suit. There was no life-sized cutout of the groom waiting for her at the end of the aisle.

Lina had to keep from looking in Petra's direction as she walked down the aisle on her father's arm. She might giggle if she caught her friend's gaze, knowing exactly what she would be thinking. Besides, it was all she could do to keep upright as, step by step, she tugged her heavy dress down the center aisle path toward her fate.

The foolish expense of the elaborate dress—which gave her the best workout in a week—was being filmed for posterity and the groom's family, who expected extravagance for their firstborn son's wedding.

The whole affair lasted less than an hour, the majority of the time spent rendering her signature on a seemingly endless pile of documents. Surprisingly, that also included receiving new identification with her married name, making her Nikolina Zupan, for the next few years, at least.

The lawyer kept shoving papers in front of her until she became almost convinced it was some ill-conceived procedure intended to further trap her in a life she wasn't certain was worth the price. But it was too late now. Lina pressed forward, signing her name over and over, even following instructions and putting her married name on a few documents toward the end of the process so she could start using it immediately.

Whatever.

They used a fax machine to expedite the official wedding document process instead of overnight mailing the papers back and forth for signatures. Another surprise, but she understood the groom's family was in a rush to ensure their son's marriage was fully processed and legal.

Lina was officially a married woman well before midnight. Nikolina Dragovic Zupan.

The date of the all-important wedding had been carefully chosen to ensure luck and good fortune for the groom.

Ironic, since Lina was a widow before the sun rose on the new day.

CHAPTER 1

A few months later – Las Vegas

Dalton Langston, beer in hand and enjoying the view from the terrace off his hotel room, kicked back on day one of a long-awaited vacation and counted his good fortune.

He had an awesome and supportive family. He had a job he loved, working at a private, ultra-exclusive security firm called The Organization. He got to travel quite a lot to various and different places as part of his day-to-day existence, a definite perk of his current occupation.

What else did he need in life to be happy and completely fulfilled? His brain zeroed in on something he'd locked away. Well, maybe there was one thing he wanted. Whether he *needed* it was open to speculation.

All of his brothers had beaten him down the aisle. Not a shock, since he was technically the youngest. Still, it prompted a few silent questions that echoed in his mind—would he ever find love? Did the perfect woman exist out there to share his life? Did he even want to settle down? Maybe. Probably. Someday.

Possibly because every single one of his older brothers had already discovered love and married amazing women, subconsciously he wanted that elusive gift as well. Or not so subconsciously.

He found himself starting to look at women a bit more speculatively, with an eye to the long-term instead of the short. So far, only one woman had made his eye linger...

Most days he loved the freedom to pick up and go where he wished with no ties on his time. Some days, however, his lifestyle seemed a lonely choice. He was very happy for his brothers and their newfound family lives. Not envious, but perhaps wishful he could find someone special to share *his* erratic life with.

Did such a woman exist? And if so, where was she?

Dalton even had a niece and nephew courtesy of his brother and sister-in-law, Reece and Jessica. Twins. Dalton's own twin, Deke, had taunted him for what felt like their whole lives as if ten years separated them instead of ten minutes.

He smiled thinking about his family, looking forward to their next biannual Key West get-together. It would be nice to attend the next gathering with a beautiful girl on his arm instead of alone.

He shook his head, banishing the reverie and put his mind in the present. He was on vacation. He was here to relax. The world was his oyster, at least for the next three weeks.

Dalton loved his work for The Organization, but he needed a break. He planned to spend the bulk of the next three weeks traveling and seeing new places before ending up in Key West for a final few days of freedom before heading back to his job. Realistically, he didn't have time to find a girl to escort to the family retreat.

But maybe if his personal project worked out…

Las Vegas wasn't new to him, as far as travel destinations went. He'd been here lots of times, but he liked it and typically made sure to visit for a few days whenever he took time off.

His fishing cabin—an RV parked perpetually in the Coyote Willow campground on Lake Havasu—was only a couple of hours drive from Vegas. He might head that way for a couple of days, too.

The last time Dalton had been there to check on his RV since his oldest brother, Alex, had used it, he'd barely opened the door and sorted through the mail before having to turn right around and leave again.

He'd pretended to be bent out of shape when his handler, Miles Turner, gave over the details of the hidey-hole for his brother's use, but he honestly didn't care. It was family.

He contemplated further places he'd like to visit, inhaling deeply and hopefully exhaling any pent-up stress from recent events.

The buzz of his phone put a frown on his face as quickly as the beer had brought the smile. Hand on his pocket, he hesitated. He was half-afraid to look at the display in case his vacation had been canceled or was some way in jeopardy of ending before it even got started.

He genuinely needed some time off to rejuvenate his soul. A flash memory of the homemade bomb strapped to his chest counting down while Alex worked feverishly to disarm it spiked his pulse for a couple of beats.

Dalton took another deep breath and exhaled before his next sip of beer sent a cool stream of relaxation to his belly.

The phone vibrated in his pocket again, signaling a text message. He pulled his phone out, looked at the display. It wasn't a number he recognized. An easy message to ignore, then. He started to tuck the phone away, but his eyes caught on the first line.

Find our missing daughter. Please, you're our last hope…

Dalton pushed out a long sigh and wished he wasn't such a sucker for the missing, especially daughters. He opened the message to read further.

The gist of the communication was a plea for help in finding a couple's missing daughter. They'd sent a file to his e-mail, which Dalton retrieved and read through to get the highlights.

Nikolina Dragovic was twenty-one when she went missing three months ago. Not exactly a missing child. The parents had employed what they called an "army" of private detectives to find her over the past few months.

A solid lead early on had traced her to Flagstaff, Arizona, sixteen hours after her disappearance, but she hadn't been seen since a security photo placed her in a bus station there. Further inquiry showed no footage of her buying a ticket. At least not at the station. It also didn't show her getting on any bus.

The attached affidavit from one detective said the parents insisted it was their daughter. No further information on that trail had been noted and the detective had apparently quit soon after, leaving no further information with regard to whether the Dragovic girl had boarded a bus or even what buses had left within the hours after the time marked on the security photo.

Sloppy work, in Dalton's humble opinion.

In a report from a different agent dated later, he read that high winds had caused a power outage to the surveillance cameras shortly after the picture was taken of the girl standing in the bus station waiting area.

There were no other pictures to verify if Nikolina had

gotten on any bus. The second agent hadn't followed up with any further reporting as to which direction Nikolina might have gone. In fact, it was the only report by this agent. More sloppy work? Interesting. Had the Dragovics hired every single bad detective agency in Arizona? The reporting of each agency had certainly been thin.

The next agency followed some vague leads in New York, but didn't mention the Flagstaff photo at all. Dalton shook his head.

The Dragovics wanted Dalton to follow up on the bus station photo and ensure everything possible had been done to find their missing child. They sounded desperate. He read the full text message again.

Find our missing daughter. Please, you're our last hope in this matter. She's our only child. A file has been sent to your e-mail address with all the information we've accumulated from an army of private detectives who brought us no results. We simply want to find out if she's still alive. Please help us.

Dalton thought it was an odd request. *We simply want to find out if she's still alive.* They didn't want her brought back? Did they want a message delivered? Did they expect her to be dead? Those points were unclear in their short e-mail and shorter text message. Maybe they didn't ask for her return because she was of age, and not a missing minor who could be compelled to go home. It made Dalton wonder what had led Nikolina to leave without telling her family where she was going. Had she been abused?

If that was the case, Dalton had firm beliefs on that score.

Or was she simply a rich young woman who wanted to do things her own way regardless of her family's wishes? Dalton recognized the Dragovic name. It was associated with wealth and social stature across the Southwest, and they were based in his hometown, Ironwood. It was also linked to criminal activity in the family's country of origin, though no Dragovic had ever been prosecuted for wrongdoing, to the best of his knowledge.

Perhaps the Dragovic girl hadn't agreed with her parents on some trivial matter and run away to be free from their rules. He had firm beliefs on that score as well. He didn't want to chase down a difficult, whiny rich girl who might just be having a tantrum. And especially not when he could be vacationing instead.

Aside from her parents' heartfelt-sounding intent, Dalton wasn't sure he wanted to involve himself in this matter. He studied the black and white photo a bit closer.

She stood alone, almost in profile. She was tiny compared to the other travelers around her, and he put her height at shorter than the average female. She wore her dark hair in a single ponytail. Although in the image, the style made her look years younger than twenty-one.

The sturdy knapsack strapped to her back looked almost as big as she was. Her posture was relaxed, her fingers wrapped around each of the backpack straps just below her collarbone, elbows tucked close to a trim body. Her gaze did not face the camera angle, her expression was not fearful or panicked, but instead wistful, or perhaps dreamy.

She wasn't smiling, but perhaps she'd been about to. One corner of her mouth barely quirked upward. Her pouty little mouth framed with lush full lips suddenly sent his baser thoughts in another direction entirely.

Shaking off an inappropriate vision, he wondered if she was satisfied she'd escaped whatever had led her away in the first place. Or had she been scheming to bend her parents to her will in some way, but been thwarted? Three months was a long time to be out of contact with one's family. He couldn't imagine it. Was she in trouble out in the world, or happy to be on her own?

Had she always intended to stay away from her parents forever or only until they agreed to her demands? Truthfully, it was difficult to glean any information from a picture months old.

Oddly enough Dalton was intrigued by what he thought was *almost* a smile to want to find out more. He stared at the photo for several minutes, feeling as though she looked a little familiar.

Had he seen her before? Perhaps he'd seen pictures of her in the news with her rich family. Or maybe not. The Dragovics had a reputation for being notoriously camera shy. Not surprising, since they were rumored to have shady ties in Kzeratia. Perhaps he only wished she looked familiar because his libido was intrigued.

The parents hadn't even sent another picture of Nikolina for comparison. They'd insisted the image was her and please go find her. Maybe he'd request a more recent photo as a stipulation of taking the case. Or maybe he'd pop open another beer and tell them he was indisposed. He was on vacation, wasn't he?

Dalton looked at the picture again as if he could figure out her intentions if only he studied her features a little longer. *Where are you, beautiful girl? Are you in trouble? Should I try to find you?*

He pushed out another long sigh, knowing that if he undertook this endeavor, it was off The Organization's books and away from his employer's extensive resources.

Dalton would be on his own, like he'd been as a bounty hunter before joining The Organization. Then again, what better way to spend his vacation than on a clandestine adventure to find the intriguing, gorgeous missing daughter of rich strangers?

CHAPTER 2

Carnival Club Casino

"You all better get your butts moving!" the line manager yelled across the kitchen in the direction of several food runners. Their shifts about to start, a group of fellow employees hovered near the time clock in an orderly row, each punching their time cards one by one and moving toward the line manager for more specific instructions.

Lina, almost at the end of her shift, had just grabbed a large, plastic wrap-covered bowl of chopped romaine to take out to the salad area. She quickly carried it from the kitchen through the swinging doors and to the buffet line at the Carnival Club Casino's main restaurant, the Big Tent Buffet.

"Emma!" a loud voice called out as soon as she emerged from the kitchen area.

The name she wore on a tag pinned to her work uniform was not her own, but was necessary to keep her true identity safe and hidden. She had quite a ways to go on reaching her new ultimate goal, but held fast to her belief that this situation wasn't forever, only for a couple of years. She'd been willing to marry someone for two years in order to change her life. In some ways, this was already better.

She was six months away from her twenty-second birthday, and two years and six months away from her long-range goal of being able to claim the funds her granny had set aside for her. The money would make the difference in her future.

Lina was working the long game. She wasn't so close to her goal that she could taste it, but planned a huge celebration a little over two and a half years from now when her plan was realized. She was certainly willing to work as hard as it took to achieve her objective.

"Emma," the floor manager called out again, motioning Lina to hurry and get the new bowl of lettuce in place for the line of hungry gamblers and guests. It was hard work physically, but she enjoyed the satisfaction of earning her way. Also, she felt safe here and that was more important than anything else at this stage of her plan.

Lina tore back the plastic on the large silver bowl one handed, grabbed the mostly empty lettuce bowl from the salad line and slipped the new full bowl in place just in time for a woman who had tongs in hand waiting for Lina to finish.

"There you go," Lina said, smiling.

The woman didn't look at her, comment or smile in return. She simply filled her generous salad plate and moved on to scoop a few sliced carrots alongside the lettuce.

Lina didn't take offense. This was exactly what she wanted—to be invisible. No one ever noticed her. No one ever talked to her. No one ever seemed to know she was alive on any given day, which was absolutely perfect.

She certainly saw her fair share of interesting people

along with quite a few handsome men, but never allowed herself to be sidetracked by anyone, especially a pretty face.

Well, there had been that time early on at this job when she saw a tall, attractive man chase a criminal out of the restaurant and then the hotel. She wished she remembered better what he looked like. At the time she'd wished for him to come back, but he hadn't. The wistful memory of him traipsed through her dreams on occasion. She was better off anyway. She didn't really remember his face after all this time—they'd only spoken for a few seconds—just that he was tall, blond and had an amazing backside.

The floor manager gestured to get her attention. "Emma! Hurry, the pickled beets are almost gone. And bring some sliced cucumbers, too. Hurry up."

Lina, the only girl runner on shift, speed-walked back toward the kitchen with the mostly empty romaine lettuce bowl pressed to her chest and the crumpled plastic wrap clutched in one hand.

Once back in the kitchen, she tossed the plastic wrap in a large lined trashcan, put the bowl on the appropriate table and sped over to the line manager. "I need pickled beets and sliced cucumbers."

The two metal bowls were thrust into her hands. Luckily they were smaller than the salad bowl and easier to manage. She glanced at the clock on the wall, heartened all the way to her weary bones by the fact her shift ended in less than twenty minutes.

Until the line manager said, "You can stay an extra hour through this rush, right, Emma?"

"Sure, no problem," she called out over one shoulder without hesitation. It hadn't taken long to get used to being called by another name.

Lina was exhausted after the first five to six hours in this job, but she *always* accepted any hours offered.

Money was constantly tight. Any added hours put her closer to her short-term goal of eking out an existence, and her long-term one of permanent freedom.

An hour and a half later, Lina brushed a stray hair away from her face with the back of one damp hand, grabbed her time card and clocked out. She accepted a generous and filling shift meal as part of her employment perks, taking her time with the luxurious food before heading home.

In this case, home was a two-bedroom, two-bathroom apartment shared by five girls of similar ages and means. There were two girls in each bedroom and one girl camping out on the sofa. The sofa camper had shown up two months ago for a single night after a breakup with her boyfriend left her temporarily homeless and she ended up staying.

That was fine with Lina. Paying one fifth of the rent was better than one fourth and the landlord didn't mind getting paid in cash, which was due every single Friday. No exceptions.

Lina didn't care who lived with her as long as they followed a few basic courtesy rules of living together and came up with their part of the rent each week. No exceptions.

The apartment was leased in the name Emma Smith, a secret ID Lina had gotten several years ago. When they'd turned sixteen, Petra's older brother had helped both of them acquire very high-end fake photo identification. He'd also garnered backup credentials to lend extra credence.

Way back when she and Petra were still in high school and all the cool parties were college-aged affairs, the ID had allowed her access to any bar or adult party she wanted entrance to. At the time, they'd each selected a fake common name so no one would necessarily remember it. Unlike Nikolina Dragovic, Emma Smith could more easily blend in and disappear into the few forbidden parties she and Petra had attended.

That fake ID had made all the difference in Lina's escape and her ability to stay hidden these last several months. She'd hinted to Petra that she'd probably go to New York, in case her friend was strong-armed into giving up some information, but Lina never intended to go east. Her destination had always been Las Vegas, or Sin City as her parents always referred to it. It seemed the perfect haven after they'd refused to give her what they'd promised.

Both her mother and father had spent a lifetime telling Lina about the horrid city in the desert, telling her she'd be brutally murdered the day she dared step one foot into such a sin-filled gambling mecca.

Reno was demonic on a smaller scale, but still a place they'd warned her never to step foot inside the city limits.

Her parents were satisfied she'd never visit a place they'd expressly forbidden, therefore, they'd never look for her in Las Vegas. They were stubborn, as she well knew.

Not telling Petra her plan to use her fake ID had been another conscious decision. She'd banked on the idea that perhaps Petra wouldn't remember it if Lina didn't bring it up and refresh her memory. She trusted her friend, but she didn't know how the other girl would stand up against threats after Lina was gone. Her parents could be very persuasive and she had a lifetime of examples in that regard.

Using her fake identification only when required and spending her dwindling and very limited cash reserves very sparingly, Lina had arrived in Las Vegas after a long bus ride from Flagstaff, rented a cheap but clean motel room for a week, and used her bogus credentials to get a job. She started as a food runner the day after she arrived in Vegas.

After a couple of days, she began to relax. She made a new friend at work who was looking for a roommate to share expenses with. Splitting the rent between the two of them in a clean, decent apartment right next to a bus stop turned out to be difficult. They'd added two more roommates to keep from simply existing paycheck to paycheck.

They still lived like poor college students. Of the five, Lina had been in town the longest at over three months. The roommate turnover every other week in the second bedroom had also served to keep Lina feeling safe from discovery. She was merely one of thousands of girls trying to make it in this town.

Each girl she lived with came with her own dreams of success. Each girl said she only planned on staying in the arrangement a few months until her ship came in, her career dream came true, or she married up to improve her financial status.

Lina didn't ever share *her* dreams, but no one seemed to care. Most girls lasted a couple of weeks before calling it quits, hating the work they had to do and giving up quickly when instantaneous success didn't happen.

Luckily, there seemed to be an endless stream of new girls looking for their big break every week. It tugged at Lina's conscience to see so many young, vulnerable girls flooding into a situation she knew from experience would not yield what they wanted. But she had enough on her plate just eking out her own existence.

Lina's plan was to stay hidden until the day she turned twenty-four. She'd take whatever money she had painstakingly saved here in Las Vegas and travel to Chicago, where her granny had banked the money. From there, the world was hers to explore and discover for as long as she had the funds to do so. Her current plan, for two-plus years from now, was to buy a one-way ticket to someplace exotic and then get a job when she ran out of money.

She wasn't too proud to work hard for a life of freedom rather than a gilded cage and another arranged husband. Especially since the new cage would likely be a permanent fixture and not a temporary home.

Lina noticed a strange car parked on the street near her apartment building and resisted the urge to duck down in her bus seat like a criminal. She wasn't a criminal, but the vehicle was rather expensive for the neighborhood.

Stranger things had happened, but she'd rather be careful than caught. Had someone tracked her down? What if someone was waiting to grab her? What if someone was ready to haul her back home?

Dalton's phone buzzed in his pocket as he considered whether he wanted to use any part of his vacation to go chasing after an extracurricular bounty.

Five years ago he would have already been on the trail as part of an initial inquiry, running through the pros and cons of what a girl like Nikolina Dragovic might be thinking as she ran and hid.

Working at The Organization had tempered his lust for being on the run all the time. It wasn't like he worked 9 to 5 there, but there was a different rhythm to working for someone else versus working alone. There were advantages and disadvantages to each path.

He glanced around the luxurious hotel room, liking what he saw. It dampened his initial enthusiasm for any off-the-books bounty hunting. It wasn't that he didn't enjoy the pursuit, but honestly, he was tired. He wanted a break. He'd come here for quiet sanctuary.

Well, and one other consideration. His personal

project. The flash of long dark hair and sultry brown eyes filtered up through his recent memory, making him reevaluate his immediate future.

Hadn't he come to Las Vegas with a certain elusive target in mind? Hadn't he wanted to discover if he could find a chance-met stranger and challenge his skills? The knowledge that his plan was not without complication, a true long shot, didn't dim his desire.

Dalton was good at finding people. Maybe he wanted to track down someone for a different purpose this time. Maybe a lucrative bounty wasn't always the best reason to look for a certain someone.

His phone buzzed again and this time he answered it, but only when he saw the familiar phone number on the display. "What!"

"Aren't you on vacation? Why would you answer your phone?" his twin demanded.

"I thought it was an emergency. You called twice."

"Nope. I only called once."

Dalton put Deke on speaker and looked at his recent phone log. An unfamiliar number was on the list as a missed call right before Deke's. Curious.

"What do you want, Deke?"

"Just checking up on you, baby brother."

Dalton rolled his eyes. It sucked being the youngest of five boys, knowing that even being a twin didn't persuade any of his siblings to label him any differently.

"You are only ten minutes older, Deke. Not ten years."

"The operative word in that sentence is 'older.' Doesn't matter by how much." His standard argument hadn't changed.

"Yeah, well, I'm taller."

Deke laughed. "Whatever helps you sleep at night, bro.

So…what are you planning to do on vacation?"

"I don't know. Fuck off. What's it to you?"

"I simply wondered if you had any special plans this time or if you were going to see anyone…special." His brother sounded strange.

Dalton huffed. "Tell you what: I promise I won't forget to look both ways before crossing the street. I won't take any candy from scary strangers in panel vans. And I'll brush my teeth every night. Can I go now, huh, can I, huh?"

Deke's warm laughter came through the phone line, making Dalton smile. Even though they could be a big pain in the ass regarding his status as the youngest, he was very close with his brothers. There wasn't anything he wouldn't do for any of them when it counted and the same was true in the reverse.

"You're going to be in Key West in a couple of weeks, though, right? The biannual gathering is coming up."

"I'm planning on it, but you never know. Sometimes my plans change without my direct consent." The notion of searching for Ivan Dragovic's daughter came into his head. Unease tickled the back of his neck at the idea of making a man with his nebulous but dark reputation the least unhappy.

He shook it off and focused on this odd conversation with his twin about the coming family reunion.

"Okay. Well, I hope you'll be here."

"Why? Is there something I need to be aware of?"

"Nope," Deke answered too quickly. "Just checking in." *Lie.* Dalton could tell by his tone that something was up. "Hoping we'll all be there together, you know." *Repeated lie. Lie. Lie.*

"What *aren't* you telling me? I can hear the anxiety in your voice."

"Oh, you cannot."

"And now you've just proved my point. What is going on? Tell me all or I will find you and make

27

you talk. You know what my skill set consists of, right?"

Deke pushed out a long, steady sigh. "Okay. Fine. I'm supposed to ask if you're bringing a plus one to Key West."

"What the hell? A plus one? I didn't know that was required."

"It's not, but I suspect if you don't bring someone with you, all the Langston wives, led by our mother, will set you up while you're here."

"What the fuck, Deke?"

"Hey, I'm just the messenger and I've already revealed too much."

Dalton rolled his eyes. Since all four of his brothers were now married, he was the only holdout bachelor in the bunch. This apparently made him a prime target for blind dates, courtesy of his loving mother and sisters-in-law.

They meant well, no doubt, but Dalton didn't believe in blind dates. He wasn't going to go on one. He didn't need any help finding a woman.

"I appreciate the warning. I didn't have plans for a plus one this trip, but now I'll ensure I bring someone with me. Thanks for the heads up, Deke."

Deke laughed again. "Oh no, you didn't hear squat from me, bro. I'm only thinking out loud and I think I accidently butt dialed your number by mistake. Have a great vacation, Dalton. No pressure on the plus one, but you're forewarned, yes?"

"Yes. Right. Got it. See you soon."

Dalton decided in that moment that he'd take a peek into the Dragovic job for his own peace of mind. He'd do a bit of checking from here, hopefully find nothing so he could call and dismiss the job.

He had a different and more personal job he'd rather attend to, especially now that a plus one might be required at the next Key West gathering.

CHAPTER 3

Lina watched carefully as the bus passed the expensive, suspicious vehicle. She pushed out a long breath when the bus's headlights shone on the license plate at the back of the car. There was no mistaking her landlord's vanity plates: 4RENT$$. He owned several apartment buildings in the area and was often on the hunt for early rent money. He must have a new car. She tried to still her racing heartbeat.

She was petrified each and every day she'd have to return to Ironwood and face difficult consequences, but she'd gotten away with her escape so far.

The memory of her last few months at home with her parents slipped into her mind like a recurring bad dream.

One day she'd been a reluctant but resigned new bride; the next, a widow stuck in an arranged proxy marriage agreement. No one was happy about any part of the situation once the groom was confirmed to be deceased.

The Zupans refused to send the major portion of the marriage settlement after their son died in a freak accident only a few hours after the ceremony. Rumors abounded that her new husband and his brother had celebrated a bit too hard after the proxy nuptials had been verified. Lina's father said the groom's stupidity wasn't his daughter's fault and demanded the agreed payment.

The whispers Lina heard involved things such as orgies in a brothel, all night clubbing to the point of excess and even a report of the groom at a hospital with irreversible alcohol poisoning. But it was all conjecture. If any part of the rumors were true, the Zupans had likely quashed any further speculation regarding their son's death.

In the nuptial agreement, Lina's parents had put in a contingency clause if the groom died before attaining his citizenship, but no one had expected him to expire within twenty-four hours of the wedding. Either way, her parents felt they'd held up their end of the bargain and the groom's post-wedding folly was his own fault and they shouldn't be punished for it.

The groom's parents disagreed. They offered their second son as a replacement for the one who'd died, but wanted additional stipulations in the marriage contract. Lina didn't want to marry again and especially not her dead husband's younger brother.

One time through the farce had been enough for her, thank you very much. At first her parents agreed, but they changed their tune when it became clear the groom's family wasn't going to budge or pay them a cent until their second son was brought over to be an eventual citizen.

Lina's parents completely disregarded her stalwart feelings on the matter and continued discussions with the Zupan family, assuming she'd simply comply with their wishes whatever transpired. They were spurred by the promised money and a proposal of more. Regardless of any other consideration, her parents were driven by the bottom line.

One night very late during the tense renegotiations,

Lina was walking past the mansion's library when she overheard her parents discussing the new marriage contract they'd received from the Zupans.

It was clear they'd learned about the money Granny Kerima planned to give her. They were discussing the wording to use in the marriage contract that would allow them to keep the money out of the Zupan groom's hands and in the Dragovic family.

Lina stood frozen next to the open door, taking it all in. That money was *hers*, not Dragovic funds to be added to the pile they already had. Besides, it wasn't millions of dollars, only a few thousand to set her on the path to freedom.

Anger unstuck her feet. She was about to waltz in and tell them the money was hers and only hers and demand they forget about it when another interesting topic arose.

The addendum the Zupan family had insisted on for the second marriage was apparently also displeasing to her parents.

"She won't agree to it," her mother said. *What won't I agree to?* Lina leaned her head as close as she dared to the doorway without spilling into the room.

"She should trust us to decide what's best for her," her father said, his booming voice getting louder as he neared the doorway. Lina inched back a bit. "I don't even like the fact that she'll be divorced one day. How can we get *that* out of the arrangement, I'd like to know. She should be more obedient."

"Pfft," her mother made a disgusted noise. "*Your* mother has put foolish ideas into Nikolina's head with that bank account she set up. Our only hope was always going to be Mislav wooing her to stay in the marriage. Now his brother will have to work even harder to achieve the same results. I'm not sure he'll be successful, given the Zupan family's new stipulations."

Lina heard her father's sigh from the hallway. "My

parents didn't have as agreeable a marriage and you and I have. My father dictated the life my mother led instead of working with her, as you and I do. A notion I wish Nikolina would adhere to regardless of her foolish defiance."

"Still, your mother should have consulted us before putting the money in Lina's name only. It changes everything. Before, we were able to *dictate* Nikolina's actions because we were the only ones offering to give her money after her duty was finished.

"With the Zupan family demanding the birth of a male child be included in the contract requirements, we'll be lucky to get her down the aisle at all. And if she discovers her husband could get custody of any account with only her name on it, she'll never agree." Her strong, cold mother was exactly right. She'd run away first. "You remember what happened with the Radovan girl and the bartender?"

Lina's father growled impatiently and she could picture him waving one arm in a dismissive slicing motion. "Yes. I remember well that horrid spectacle. It doesn't matter. Nikolina will have to agree to give the second Zupan boy a son in order to appease his parents. Nothing else will be accepted for their joining."

"Then we must keep that stipulation from her until the second proxy wedding is performed and she's bound by contract."

Lina eased away from the doorway with a sense of shock. *A child? Or rather a boy child before she'd be released to leave?* No. That would tie her to the marriage for longer than three years and complicate the intended divorce immeasurably. She couldn't bear the thought of being forced to bring a child of hers into either family. They would both be trapped and the cycle would continue.

"How can we get her *not* to read the new contract?" her father asked.

"I don't know. She insisted on reading every word of the last one."

Numbly, Lina listened as her parents continued to discuss ways to hide the additional demand from her. They were determined to find a way. If Lina didn't sign the agreement to marry the Zupan heir *and* to produce a son in the next three years, they'd fail to secure the second marriage document and, most importantly to them, lose out on all the promised money they stood to receive.

Finally, her mother said, "We'll simply tell her the agreement is the same with the addition of a year of mourning. Just bring her the signature page and say it's the only change. Once she signs it, she can't back out. You're right, we're her parents. She should trust us."

Her parents coldly deciding not to tell her about either the required male child or that her money might be in jeopardy angered her, but their planned deception in getting her to sign a new contract without disclosing the information horrified her.

Lina went straight to her room, gathered the cash she'd secreted away to spend on things her parents disapproved of, stuffed her fake ID, the documents from her marriage and some clothes in a backpack, and run away that very night. She headed straight for Petra's home to bid her farewell and ask for help. She needed transportation away from town.

They had conspired all night to get Lina far away from Arizona as soon as possible. Lina wasn't worried her parents would notice she was missing. They wouldn't think to look for her until they needed her to sign the new documents, and she was certain they had to go to the lawyers first. She had a bit of time to plan. Her worst regret was leaving her best friend, knowing she might never see Petra again.

Lina snapped back to the present as the bus hissed and groaned, slowing near her stop. She was the only one who stepped off. She was barely through the opening before the doors slammed shut with a snap behind her and the bus rumbled away to its next destination.

She headed to her three story apartment building, carefully stepping over the weed-framed, broken and cracked concrete of the sidewalk along the way to her first floor apartment.

After her extra-long shift, all she wanted to do was crawl in bed and sleep. Not having to climb a flight or two of stairs was a grateful bonus Lina appreciated each and every time she returned home from a long day at work.

She unlocked and opened the door to her apartment and was greeted with the frantic noise level that having five girls living together created on any given evening.

The television was on, music was blaring from another direction, a blow-dryer was blasting in the bathroom and something was burning in the kitchen. Of the three girls Lina could see, all stared at their phones with rapt attention.

"Hey," she called out to the chaos, not expecting an answer.

The girl watching television, but really staring at her phone, looked up briefly to say, "Hey."

"Anything exciting going on?" Lina asked, as she did every night. Typically, if she got any answer at all it was a shrug and more often there was no sign she'd even spoken. Wasted breath.

Tonight, she was surprised when Chrissy said, "There was some guy looking for you a little while ago." She turned back to her screen as if she'd merely commented on the weather.

To say horror choked Lina was a ludicrous understatement. Fear blazed down her spine in an instant. She fought it back.

Wait. The rent was due in three days. Her landlord was on the prowl in the area, probably seeking money. She unclenched, exhaled and asked, "Was it the landlord looking for our rent money early again?"

Never once looking up from her phone, and thumb typing the whole time, her roommate said, "No, a stranger."

The terror returned. Her belly roiled. The rich, filling meal from work settled unevenly in her stomach. "What did he look like?" she asked, trying to keep the fear out of her tone. Was it her father? Was it someone her family sent to retrieve her?

It certainly wasn't any type of suitor looking for an evening out. Lina had purposely stayed away from men, *all* men, while living here. She hadn't so much as glanced at an attractive man—save for one very brief exception—unless she was assured he didn't see her, never wanting attention, never wanting to be found out.

"Um…" Chrissy held her mouth open as if about to respond but didn't continue.

"Hey, what did he look like?" Lina asked again, harshly.

Chrissy pushed out a disgusted sigh and took her focus briefly away from her phone to stare at Lina. "Chill, okay? He was a super tall, blond surfer-dude hottie with intense gray-blue eyes wanting to talk to Emma Smith from Arizona, okay?" She dropped her gaze back to her phone, adding absently, "Are you from Arizona? I thought you came from New York."

CHAPTER 4

Dalton finished his beer and headed down to the hotel business center office to log on to his remote account to do an initial hunt for the elusive Nikolina Dragovic. He'd left his laptop at home, since he'd be on vacation for the next few weeks. He should have known better.

Nikolina's parents didn't believe she could possibly be in Las Vegas, as they'd made it clear to their daughter it was a sin-filled place where girls like her were either killed outright or worse, if not immediately sold into slavery the moment they stepped into town. Not a misguided fairytale, as it was certainly possible, but not an outright truth either.

Dalton figured if this girl had any smarts, Las Vegas was the first place she'd go. He decided to do a thorough search of the Las Vegas area, since he was right here anyway. Then he'd head to New York, where her parents thought she was. If the Vegas search didn't pan out, he wouldn't charge them for his time here. They likely wouldn't pay for any wasted time in Sin City anyway, given how they'd treated former agencies for even suggesting what they called "a big waste of time."

The files Dalton had initially received earlier from the parents turned out not to be complete, but a summary. He received a second and more complete set of documents and reread through the more detailed reports made by the many previous private detectives. Most *had* done a pretty decent job, given the constraints imposed by the parents. And lucky for him, they'd taken very good notes. Unlucky for them, the moment they mentioned Las Vegas or Reno as a possible location, they'd been fired.

Dalton hadn't officially agreed to take the case, but he sent word he'd think about it. If he couldn't figure out where she might have gone in a couple of hours, he might simply tell her parents, "Sorry, I'm not available at this time." He was interrupting his vacation after all. And the only reason he wanted to do anything at all was to see what the girl in the dark ponytail looked like in person. Not the best reason, perhaps, but she was the one who intrigued him, not her parents' offer.

Dalton retraced the steps taken by the other agencies to form his own conclusions regarding where the elusive Nikolina Dragovic might have gone.

Nikolina's best friend had been questioned by all of the detectives. Her statement had remained unchanged. After some pressure, she'd intimated that "Lina" had always wanted to go to New York.

The possibility of an arranged marriage came up, but the parents denied it. The careful wording and starred notation in each and every report where it was mentioned told Dalton Lina's parents were probably lying. If they lied about why she'd left, what else were they lying about?

The first investigation service asked the Dragovics why they thought their daughter had run off. The parents had not been very forthcoming, but later notes in a margin by the detective said they'd been hiding something. No shocker there. Lots of people lied for lots of reasons. The arranged marriage idea surfaced during the second detective's search and then in subsequent agency fact-finding missions.

Dalton figured there was either some truth to it or they'd at least threated their daughter with it. That was a better reason for Nikolina to have "scurried away in the dead of night," as her parents had worded it.

One detective had gotten hold of the names of all bus ticket holders in the Flagstaff station an hour before and after the picture had been timestamped. The expansive list was included, but eight buses left in the hour after that picture had been taken and four had left the station in the second hour, giving a whopping list of nearly three hundred names or approximately twenty-five people per bus. No Nikolina Dragovic had been listed on any manifest, naturally.

And even *that* assumed she'd purchased a ticket using her own name. Someone could have purchased the ticket for her. Or she had a fake ID. Or she'd been at the bus station seeing someone else off. It was unlikely, but still a consideration. Maybe Lina was hiding back in Arizona right under their noses.

Dalton studied the list and read the notes. The detective had only gone through about the first half of the list, seeking women under the age of thirty who'd been traveling alone. He'd made several cold calls without any result to people who didn't remember noticing a young woman of Lina's description or appreciate receiving the calls in the first place.

Apparently the detective had given up before contacting all the names on the list, and he hadn't even bothered to check the passengers on the bus going to Las Vegas, as per the parents' insistence. He'd strenuously disagreed with them on that point and been fired. The case had been handed to yet another agency a few days later. Perhaps that was why the remaining names on the list hadn't been contacted.

So Dalton decided to finish the job, but he'd start with the Las Vegas list and see if any of those passengers were still in the city three months later.

It was a stretch, but he was already here. Out of the thirty-one passengers on the bus to Vegas, only fourteen were women. Even if he didn't find Lina, perhaps someone seated on the bus during that trip might remember the young woman in the picture.

A basic search—basic to him—found that four of the female passengers were current residents in the Las Vegas area. He looked at the picture again, torturing himself by staring at her.

Dalton thought she was quite striking, even in a black and white photo with her hair up in a ponytail. Her mouth still made wicked things pop into his head, so he tucked the picture back in his pocket to stop obsessing. He couldn't shrug off the sense there was something familiar about her.

He shook his head and got down to business. He had four addresses to check out. He mapped their locations, then reordered the names and addresses for optimal efficiency from his current location and the desire to not spend the entire night in busy Las Vegas traffic.

First up, he'd visit Emma Smith. She'd purchased a one-way ticket to Las Vegas and paid with cash less than an hour before leaving Flagstaff.

He found more than one Emma Smith in Las Vegas, but access to a handy database he tapped into with additional information listed one Emma Smith as a resident for only the past three months and she also fit the approximate age group.

Ostensibly he was looking for anyone who'd seen the girl in the black and white picture, but his gut said one of these four women might actually *be* Nikolina

Dragovic. That could simply be wishful thinking on his part.

If he didn't find his target in Las Vegas—and after thinking about it, he didn't expect this job to be that easy—perhaps he'd take on the daunting task of looking for her in New York. Or he'd beg off and resume his vacation. His future plans were a toss-up at the moment.

Dalton tried to put himself in Lina's place. She was possibly escaping her parents and a Draconian arranged marriage. She had been fairly sheltered or possibly cut off from the staples of regular teen life, as he'd found no social media information even from when she'd lived at home. She was currently on the run, likely using a fake name, possibly hiding in a place she expected her parents not to search.

His understanding was that she hadn't been able to bring much money with her. She'd left her purse behind with her identification inside it. Her parents told all of the previous detectives that she didn't even have a driver's license.

Out in the world with limited cash and no driver's license, she'd be forced to make difficult decisions. And if she had assumed the name of Emma Smith or one of the other names on his list, she'd still need a valid social security card to find legitimate employment.

If not, her choice of jobs was limited even further.

Dalton did a quick background check on Emma Smith of Las Vegas. No outstanding warrants. No tickets. Also, no driver's license, but that wasn't completely unexpected. If she didn't have money for a car, perhaps a license was an unnecessary expense.

There was nothing about where she'd come from before arriving in Sin City. There was a home address listed and her work address was the Carnival Club Casino. He often stayed at that hotel, although not this particular trip. The last time, oddly enough, was about three months ago. He'd been chasing an elusive criminal with extraordinarily good luck.

After showing a photo to a restaurant worker, a girl with long dark hair had pointed out the man Dalton sought. The criminal looked up and saw Dalton and the girl watching him and he'd taken off at a dead run. Dalton chased him out of the restaurant, through the casino and ended up running after the loser down the Vegas strip like in an action movie.

Turned out the guy had spent an inordinate amount of time in one of the casino buffet restaurants, as if that crowded space would keep him permanently hidden. It hadn't. Dalton found him there.

Thinking about the pretty worker at the casino buffet reminded him he should get at it, and go see her possible co-worker, Emma Smith. If he didn't find her at home, he'd try her at work. If Emma Smith didn't look anything like the girl in the picture, he'd move on to the next name. His gut was telling him she was his best candidate on the short list he carried.

Gut feelings, as he well knew from experience, could be wildly mistaken.

Lina marched over to her roommate, Chrissy, and snatched her phone from her rapidly moving fingers. "Pay attention to me."

"Hey, give that back!" Chrissy's eyes stared longingly at her phone. The two other girls within view, one in the kitchen hovering over a still smoking toaster and the other at the kitchen table, didn't even look up from their phones.

"Tell me everything about the man who came here looking for me. What's his name? When was he here?"

"I don't know exactly when he was here." She

glanced at her phone again. "Not very long ago, I think."

The girl reached for her cellular, but Lina held it out of reach. "His name, please?"

Chrissy looked wildly around the room. "I don't know, but he left a card or something."

"What card? A business card?"

"I guess. It's on the counter over there." She pointed at the kitchen bar and snatched her phone back, resuming typing as if her life depended on it. Lina mentally rolled her eyes and went in search of the stranger's card.

She found it easily, picked it up and read, "Dalton Langston, Security Specialist." Below the name was a number with an Arizona area code. Damn it. Was she caught already after only a few months? Had her parents hired someone to look for her in Las Vegas after all?

It would be a big surprise and a huge miscalculation on her part. They'd drilled into her head that Las Vegas was a place no girl should ever travel to for any reason and most especially never alone. Petra had some distant cousins in Las Vegas. They had managed to survive regardless of their gender. True, that branch of Petra's family was the Dragovics' rivals in the shady family business department. That was the most likely reason her parents didn't want her here, but Lina felt safe enough as long as no one learned she was a Dragovic.

Dread coated her insides as she gripped Dalton Langston, Security Specialist's card tight in her fingers. Taking a deep breath and giving a long exhale to calm down, Lina considered what she should do.

If he had a picture, her disguise might not hold up to careful scrutiny. She'd cut her long dark hair and lightened the color shortly after arriving in Vegas. The blue-colored contact lenses had been expensive, but also helped conceal her appearance.

She started coloring her hair black at thirteen, not

wanting her light hair to stand out in a sea of dark-haired relatives. That had worked for her in this instance. Maybe no one would consider she'd go back to her golden blond.

Lina changed out of her uniform and into jeans and a T-shirt. She left the apartment for the library only a few blocks away. Glancing at the time, she hurried her steps. She had less than an hour before it closed for the night.

She should still have plenty of time to get online and look up Dalton Langston. It would be helpful if she could find out what *he* looked like. Then if she saw him coming, she could be better prepared. Perhaps along with the ugly plastic head cover she wore at work, she'd also adopt the odd custom of wearing a mask like a surgeon to keep her identity even safer.

A smile surfaced at the ridiculousness of that. She often wore disposable plastic gloves at work along with her plastic hair cover, but a mask might make her look sick. Not an acceptable vision for dining establishments.

The library's sliding glass doors swished open as she approached, admitting her into one of her favorite places in town. In her limited free time, she found sanctuary here, hiding away in the aging building, enjoying the distinct scent of books collected together.

Lina approached the public computer area, searching for an open desk. She found one at the very end of the first row. She logged on, selecting a well-known search engine to look for Mr. Langston in Arizona.

She got more than she bargained for. Clicking on images for Langstons in Arizona, she saw several pictures of an attractive man who'd apparently thwarted several attempted kidnappings and even a murder, but it was the wrong Langston. Deke Langston—not Dalton—was a bodyguard who'd saved a rather famous movie star from some vicious stalker. Maybe Deke and Dalton were brothers.

She scanned the array of pictures and found a more recent news story regarding a bomb threat in Ironwood, Arizona, where a bomb technician and firefighter named Alex Langston had rescued his brother, Dalton, from a homemade explosive vest.

The photo of Dalton was from a distance, but she could see he was very tall compared to the firefighters and police officers standing near him. His face was toward the camera, but the image wasn't large enough to see much detail. He did have dark blond hair. She couldn't tell what color his eyes were, but figured it was the same Dalton Langston who'd come looking for her.

Lina tried another search attempting to find a better photo, but Dalton was apparently as secretive as she was regarding social media. She didn't find any other pictures of him anywhere public.

She looked at the singular photo she'd found once more, studying his tall, muscular, beautiful body. Height challenged, as many in her family were, Lina was only five foot four, if she stretched her spine to the maximum possible extent.

Dalton Langston was easily three or four inches above six feet. Her roommate Chrissy had said the man was blond, tall and a surfer-dude hottie. She was right. Reviewing the photo carefully, Lina figured the top of her head likely wouldn't even come up to his wide shoulders. He did look a bit like a surfer with his wavy dark blond hair.

His facial features were not distinct in the faraway photo, but Lina had the funny feeling she might have seen this man before.

Had he been a customer at the Big Tent Buffet? Had he been one of the literally thousands of people she'd seen filling endless plates with all the food she carried out to replenish the buffet for most of the past three months? Surely not.

What were the odds? Lina smiled suddenly. *That* particular question likely got asked quite often in Las Vegas. What *were* the odds of a man looking for her after seeing her at the casino where she worked? Maybe better than average.

Before she could contemplate any further whether she'd ever seen Dalton Langston, hot surfer-dude-looking Security Specialist, one of the librarians came around to announce the library would be closing in fifteen minutes.

She twirled the business card in her fingers and wondered if she should simply call him and ask what he wanted. If it turned out to be her worst fear, she'd grab her skimpy nest egg and bolt.

Lina logged off the library's computer and headed for the exit. Head down, carefully watching the uneven sidewalk ahead, she walked at as fast a clip as she dared. She stuffed her hands in the pockets of the light jacket she wore against the slight chill in the evening air and started back to her apartment to do some serious thinking about what she'd say if she got up the nerve to call.

Maybe coming to Las Vegas had been a bad idea. Or maybe she'd tested fate long enough here in Sin City. Had she underestimated her parents? Should she grab her pitiful stash from the hiding spot in her room and hightail it to Chicago now instead of waiting for another two years?

She'd planned to save up enough to live in a cheap motel for approximately two months upon her arrival to the windy city in Illinois. Too bad she still needed to save up another ninety percent of her goal as of today. She also expected a possible delay to collect her funds even after her twenty-fourth birthday, which was why she planned to wait until after her birthday to get any paperwork started. It wouldn't do not to have money saved up in case the funds weren't immediately accessible.

Plus, whenever she *did* go to Chicago, she didn't plan on going to the bank right away. Her parents knew about the account, so they would likely have someone waiting there for her. A certainty, since she'd disappointed them by not staying around to be duped into a second marriage.

Her mind went to how much she could economize in Chicago and still eat on a daily basis. This train of thought only made her more desperate. She didn't have nearly enough saved. She'd last a week, maybe. She'd have to find another place to live and another low-key job to survive. Not impossible, but not in her plans. Her current arrangement had been perfect and the thought of having it threatened now angered her.

Pushing out a sigh, Lina tried to calm down. She didn't have enough money to go yet, and she knew it.

If only Mr. Dalton Langston hadn't shown up on her doorstep with his business card.

Lina was a block from her apartment when she heard some kind of skirmish behind her. She kept walking.

It wasn't unheard of for fights or any number of scuffles to break out on the streets of any city, especially Las Vegas. This wasn't the best neighborhood, but a scuffle was only a problem if the men were after her. Were they here following her? A chill ran down her spine for the second time tonight. Lina sped her steps, too afraid to look back and find out if someone was chasing her or, worse, gaining on her.

She was so focused on getting home without being caught that she didn't notice the large, looming figure lingering near the tall hedges by the pathway leading to her apartment building.

"Nikolina," a man's deep, unfamiliar voice said from the darkness.

CHAPTER 5

Dalton hadn't strayed too far from Emma Smith's apartment after speaking to her roommate. He was walking slowly toward his vehicle, parked further down the street and out of sight, when he looked over his shoulder and saw a petite blonde get off a bus at the stop in front of the building.

He'd planned to sit in his car for a little while and watch for anyone matching Nikolina Dragovic's description, but then the blonde started walking toward the apartment building.

He ducked out of sight, watching to see if she approached the building. Not only did she approach the building he'd visited with slow, tired steps, she walked right up to Emma Smith's door on the first floor and entered with a key.

Interesting. He pulled the black and white Flagstaff picture out of his pocket, illuminating it with the light from his phone, trying to see if it resembled the girl he'd seen—as if he hadn't already memorized every line and curve in that photo.

Even with shorter blond hair, it was her. No doubt in his mind.

Nikolina Dragovic had been living as Emma Smith in

Las Vegas for over three months, the last place her parents expected her to be. So, she was a smart girl after all.

One of his initial worries was that since she hadn't come back after a week of abject poverty, perhaps something unexpected had happened to her. Everything he'd read in the files said she didn't have much money. Her parents didn't seem to think she had the wherewithal to live without help for very long. Perhaps someone had taken pity on her or her parents had underestimated her.

His respect for her ability to remain hidden all these months doubled. But he still had a job to do. Dalton pondered how he'd approach her now that he'd found her. Should he beat around the bush about why he was here? Show her the photo and ask if she recognized the dark-haired girl with the ponytail from a three-month-old picture?

Would she run? Would he chase her? Yes.

He hid in the shadows, letting "Emma" get herself settled inside her apartment before knocking on the door again. He wanted to catch her unaware regardless of what plan he enacted. But before he could even finish making a strategy, the girl in question raced back out of the apartment and headed in the opposite direction down the street.

Dalton almost gave chase. Where was she going? Was she running away? He held himself back. She didn't even have any luggage or a purse. No, not running. She was too smart for that.

She was up to something else. Time to chase, but not overtly.

Dalton followed her at a discreet distance, wondering if his visit had spurred her action. She led him a few blocks away to a well-lit public library. He followed her inside, careful to ensure she didn't see him.

She must have dyed her hair, although it looked

amazingly real. The color was a dark blonde with golden streaks and not unlike his own hair when he spent the entire summer in the sun.

Lina stopped suddenly, looking around as if someone might be following her. Dalton ducked into a tall row of shelves housing books on biographies, grabbing the first book he saw and opening it to peruse intently as if he couldn't wait another moment to discover the details of Albert Einstein's life story. Through the space between the shelf and tops of the books he hid behind, Dalton saw Lina move toward an area at the back with tables and the public computers.

Carrying the biography along with him, in case he needed to pretend he was absorbed in Einstein's theory of relativity, Dalton eased himself away from the biography row and sauntered toward a shelf near Lina.

He casually strolled behind where she sat in front of a computer, watching her intently. He saw his business card clutched in her delicate fingers and quickly hid behind a rack of magazines to watch. It soon became clear that she was looking *him* up online.

Interesting. Actually, she hadn't found him yet. Dalton saw a familiar and rather famous picture of Deke on her computer screen, directly after his twin had thwarted a stalker in a high-profile movie star's case. She clicked on several links bringing up articles from Ironwood, Arizona, including one not long ago involving Dalton, his brother Alex and a homemade bomb vest. She *was* looking him up.

Dalton's respect for her doubled yet again. She was very smart.

He wasn't certain if she would find a picture of him. He was careful about such things, but it wasn't easy to keep hidden in the surveillance-filled world they all lived in these days.

Dalton looked around the library. There were few people and most of them were headed out the door. On the way in he'd noted the place was about to close. Fortunately, no one seemed to notice him staring at the beautiful girl he'd followed into the library. But there was no sense pushing his luck.

With one last glance at her back, he memorized her build, noting he liked her as a blonde as well as when she'd sported dark hair in Flagstaff. Dalton laid the Einstein biography on the first table he came to, took a roundabout way to a side exit and left the library. He wondered how to approach her now. He stared into the library's front window. She was still seated at the computer.

What was his plan in case she discovered a picture of him and knew what he looked like? Chase her faster when next they met?

She'd obviously gotten the business card he left with one of her many roommates, although the girl he'd spoken to never took her eyes far from her phone the entire time he was at the door.

He couldn't wait to see what Lina did next. Would she run for it? Grab what cash she had on hand and bolt for the great unknown? Wait for him to show up? Call him? Probably not.

Dalton had already established the fact she was smart, which meant she wouldn't leave the city unless she had to. Her parents had mentioned a time limit in their email, but he hadn't discovered that exact date yet. Maybe she was also waiting for that unspecified date before she could act.

He didn't know what her goals were, or what her parents' plans were. Truth be told, his clients' plans shouldn't matter to him in the least. He was paid not to care, but in this instance, for some inexplicable reason, he did. Well, thinking about her new hair color and her smart actions at the library, maybe the reason was *explicable* after all.

Dalton was already rooting for Lina to succeed, which was completely at odds with his current agenda. He'd only promised to look into the case to decide whether or not to take it, all the time planning on searching Las Vegas first due to proximity and his gut hunch.

A glance at his watch and a check on his phone told him she'd have to leave the library in less than five minutes or get locked in overnight.

Careful to stay far enough away to remain out of her view when she came out of the building, Dalton hunkered next to a hedge beside a business that had closed for the day. The pungent, fetid stench of a garbage Dumpster was somewhere close by, making him want to find a new place to hide.

He breathed through his mouth—which was only marginally better—and watched for his quarry.

He didn't have to wait for long. She came out through the front doors and headed in the direction of her apartment building. She wasn't moving as fast this time. He let her walk past his hiding place, counting to ten slowly in his head before standing up to follow her home.

Dalton rounded the hedge, gratefully leaving behind the nasty smell of ripe trash, and walked toward the street leading back to Nikolina "Lina" Dragovic, A.K.A. Emma Smith's, apartment.

Following half a block behind her careful steps, Dalton kept his eyes focused on the back of her head. He thought through what he'd say to her, what he'd do if she turned and saw him or tried to run. He didn't want to frighten her.

His best option was to call her parents and tell them where she was, but he wasn't ready to do that. Maybe he'd back off a bit and wait until she got inside her apartment. He could knock on the door and say her parents sent him because they were worried. Perhaps he'd listen to her side of the story before assessing what to do.

Plus, he needed to ensure she truly *was* Nikolina before doing a single thing. And it didn't hurt that she intrigued him to no end and had since he'd studied the black and white picture from the bus station earlier today and registered that she looked familiar.

Part of him deep down wondered at his quick success in finding her. It was really too easy. He'd always been a very good tracker of people. It was why he'd done so well as a bounty hunter once upon a time. But was he really *this* good?

Watching the sway of her blond hair and the way she walked made him want to like everything about her. He resisted the urge to grin like an idiot after his dream girl.

Lina was a block away from home, still walking at her slow pace in that direction. If that was her intended destination, perhaps he should speed up, take an alternate path and run ahead to beat her there. Dalton maintained his distance half a block behind her, but he increased the length of his stride in an effort to catch up.

If he could get ahead of her without being seen, he would wait on the sidewalk in front of her apartment. Or perhaps he would let her get inside her apartment and then knock on her door. Yes, a better plan.

If she didn't recognize him, or immediately tried to slam the door in his face, he'd show her the picture and give her his spiel regarding the search for a missing girl, mention her worried parents and see how she reacted.

She only had a few more steps until she was back at her building's front walkway. He wouldn't get ahead of her. Rethinking his plan as to what to say to her, Dalton was unprepared for something hard and painful to slam against the back of his head.

He saw stars and dropped to his knees. Black blotches crowded his vision and then nothing.

Lina turned at the sound of her name, immediately angry with herself for responding to a name she hadn't used in months. She'd been Emma Smith since boarding the bus to Las Vegas, so why did her old name still make her jump when called?

A tall man stepped from the high hedge shadows. Was it the man she'd been researching at the library?

"Mr. Langston?" she asked quietly.

The man stepped into the partial light. She could see only half of his sharply angled, handsome face. A smile surfaced on the side of his mouth that she could see in the dimness as he approached her slowly. He was fairly tall, maybe an inch over six feet, but not as tall as she'd expected him to be.

"Why are you looking for me?" she asked a little louder. "Who sent you?" She wondered briefly if he could be bought off or bribed, although she didn't have enough money to do either of those things.

"Nikolina," he said again in such a low tone she had to listen carefully to hear the rest of what he said. "You've led me on a rather long chase. Don't you think it's time for you to come home and do your duty?"

"No. I don't. There is nothing for me there. Besides, I already did my duty." Lina's belly roiled with unhappiness.

First, she was afraid she'd been followed from the library and now this man blocked her path to her apartment. Obviously, he'd been sent by her parents.

"That's not true, Nikolina," his voice had risen barely

above a whisper, but it was enough for her to register an accent. It was a familiar inflection, sounding much like her grandparents' distinctive voices.

"Who are you?" she asked, suspicion coating her wary tone.

He stopped moving. His head cocked to one side, as if her words puzzled him. "You know who I am. You already said my name."

"You aren't Mr. Langston."

Without warning, the man lunged, grabbing her forearm in one strong hand. She tried to pull away, but his steely grasp tightened painfully. She parted her lips to scream, but he clamped his free hand over her mouth and pushed her into the waist-high hedge lining the walkway to her apartment building.

The stranger's body pushed into her, backing her against the dense foliage. Limbs snapped and poked her in the back as he crushed her against the hedge. The scent of his strong, sweet, musky cologne nearly choked her. The stranger pressed her into near immovable submission against the foliage. She needed to do something drastic and she needed to do it now. Lina's mind spun wildly in panic. Against every innate sense she possessed, Lina stopped fighting. She went limp.

Her sudden lack of resistance threw the man off balance. He loosened his grasp, only slightly, and she took advantage. She pushed him with all her might and, lifting her leg hard and fast, connected her knee solidly between his legs.

Lina's bent leg dropped away and he released her to use his hands to cover the place she'd just kneed hard. He made a squealing sort of grunt and fell to the sidewalk, landing in a partial fetal position, whimpering.

She didn't pause to give her attacker a chance to recuperate. She ran for her life back toward the library. She'd only gone half a dozen steps when she saw a very tall man fighting off three other men. He was doing a pretty good job. In the light of an overhead streetlamp, she saw the tall man had blond hair.

She slowed, but kept moving in that direction, unwilling to go back to the man she'd hurt. Could the tall man be Dalton Langston? Lina heard an odd, indefinable noise behind her and hurried her steps toward the unfair fight, vowing to help the underdog in the short term.

She didn't want to go back to the man she'd kicked. He'd be all kinds of angry and after her with a vengeance when he could walk again. Lina was more frightened of him because he knew her real name. If he wasn't Dalton Langston, who else was after her?

The tall man elbowed the biggest of his foes in the face with a solid jab, sending the guy sprawling to the ground, where he stayed. The heavier of the remaining two attackers bashed the tall blond in the lower back. The underdog in this unfair fight swayed on his feet at first and then went to his knees. The heavy man rained more punches down on top of him.

The third attacker also moved closer, pummeling the tall man with savage and repeated body blows. By the time she got close enough to do anything to help, the tall man had his arms over his head as he took four fists worth of punches to his forearms, chest and back.

That's totally unfair.

Lina saw a three-foot long dead limb in the grass, beneath an equally dead tree. It was the size of her wrist and looked like a viable weapon. She grabbed it up on her way to the fray. Moving close to the men, she lifted the branch like a baseball bat and swung as hard as she could at the head of the heaviest guy. He crumpled to the ground.

Reprieved, the tall man got back up like he'd merely been resting as they hammered repeated hits on him, and punched the remaining guy in the jaw. The last attacker went down without a single noise.

The tall man turned to her and she got a good look at his amazingly handsome, if battered, face. The moment his gaze landed on her, his eyes widened. Was he surprised to see a girl had helped him? He was clearly the guy she'd seen in that picture online based on his size. Dalton Langston. He was several inches over six feet. There was a streak of dirt or blood across his forehead and a scratch along his jaw. But still, he was very nice to look at. And also familiar.

"Are you Mr. Langston?"

"Yes. Thanks, for stepping in when you did."

"Didn't seem like a fair fight, but you probably didn't need me."

His sudden grin made him even more attractive, and Lina swore she heard angels sing. "It wasn't a fair fight. But I was caught off guard. You definitely helped me. My manly pride dictates that I tell you I'm usually better against three guys. Not so much today. I owe you one."

"Well, the cowardly blows to your back when you were already down probably put you off your game. You don't owe me," she said as she watched him. He stared back intensely. She liked it, but should stop mooning over him to find out what he wanted.

"Right. Thanks again."

"Why are you looking for me, Mr. Langston?" she asked, wanting to assess his danger level to her, mindful of the man she'd left behind clutching his privates. She pulled his business card from her pocket and waved it, unwilling to give it back.

"Please, call me Dalton." *My, oh my.* He was *very* nice to look at and his voice made her feel all melty inside. *Pay attention.*

"Okay, Dalton. Same question."

"I have a picture to show you, Miss Smith."

Silently, Lina pushed out a breath of relief. Maybe he didn't know her real name. Maybe her disguise was working. It was a fleeting hope because the other man who'd grabbed her had called her by her real name. Someone after her knew who she really was.

He reached inside his inner jacket pocket and pulled a photo out, handing it to her. She wanted to touch his hand, but it would have been too obvious. She stared down at the dog-eared photo.

The black and white picture was of her back at the Flagstaff bus station right before she'd come here. Her hair had been dark and in a long ponytail. It seemed like a decade had passed since that naive girl came to Las Vegas looking to be invisible.

"I wondered if you remembered seeing this woman on your bus journey to Las Vegas three months ago," he said. His gaze never left her. She stared into his eyes, searching for the truth. And found it. He knew *exactly* who she was.

"Let's not play any more games." Lina held the photo up to her face, gesturing with a sweep of her fingers at the likeness between them. "Who paid you to find me?"

An expression that looked strangely like admiration covered his features for a brief moment. "Your parents. They wanted me to find out if you're still alive. They said I was their last hope."

"I see. Well, I *am* still alive." In the distance, a dog barked. "I *hope* you are the last one to look for me, but that would be a foolish thing to believe on my part since you obviously aren't working alone." Lina looked behind her in the general direction of her apartment. She couldn't go back there. "You and your friend can tell my parents to leave me alone."

"Friend? What friend?"

She pointed a thumb over her shoulder toward her apartment building, where she'd left the guy on the ground. "The guy who tried to grab me back at my apartment. He mentioned I needed to go home to do my duty. I'm not interested. I already did my duty."

"I don't know anything about anyone's duty or yours in particular. Also, I absolutely always work alone," Dalton said rather passionately. "If you saw another guy, he wasn't with me. This is the first time I'm hearing about taking you anywhere. I was only asked to find you and whether you were alive, but the truth is I hadn't even accepted the job yet."

Lina loved the sound of his voice. She loved that he was so tall. She shook off her lust. Her parents would insist she marry again if she ever went home. Lina wasn't certain to what extent they'd go to ensure she complied. She'd learned the hard way that her own flesh and blood didn't have her best interests at heart. She needed to remember that this attractive man likely didn't have her best interests at heart either. "I see. And now that you've found me, will you take the job?"

"I'm not certain yet. I was told not to bother looking for you in Las Vegas as it would be a waste of my time and their money." He gave her another grin that melted her insides faster than she'd ever be willing to admit out loud. Where was her cautionary inner voice?

Lina nodded, trying to cover her attraction. What he said about Las Vegas sounded exactly like what her parents would say. That was why she was here. "Who are these guys at our feet?" she asked, wondering if more people than just her parents were after her. And had found her.

"No clue. Do you know the name of the other guy?"

She looked over her shoulder again, hoping not to see the man she'd kicked, and shook her head. "Actually, when I said your name he pretended to be you."

Dalton frowned and moved a step closer. Was this a protective streak? If so, she liked it. A moment of girly admiration rose within. She wished she had someone like Dalton for protection. Someone to share the burden of her secrecy. The life she'd been living in Las Vegas was a difficult one, not to mention lonely. She looked at his muscular body, surprised by how attracted she was to him. That whisper of familiarity wound its way back into her consciousness. *Have I seen him before?* She searched her memory.

"Is anyone besides your parents after you?" he asked, breaking her reverie.

She shrugged. "I have no idea."

"How tall was he? Any distinguishing marks?"

She shook her head. Then stopped. "He *did* have an accent, and I'm fairly certain it's Kzeratian or possibly Russian, but I'm not a dialect expert." She feared it was Kzeratian and they'd found her. He'd sounded like the memory of her strict grandfather Dragovic.

His brows narrowed. "I don't know anyone with a Russian accent or a Kzeratian one either."

"Good. Because he grabbed me very hard and frightened me." Her eyes filled with tears as she remembered how instantly terrified she'd been when the man had pushed her into the hedge. She wanted to go back to her apartment, but didn't feel safe enough to return there.

As if he read her mind, Dalton said, "Don't be upset. I'll escort you to your apartment, if you'd like."

"What if he's still there?" The sudden concern in his eyes told her he'd heard the panic in her tone. "I kicked him—you know—hard in a very bad place where men don't like to be kicked. He'll be furious with me."

Dalton's head tilted to one side, but he didn't say anything at first, as if mulling the idea of what she'd done to a fellow male's family jewels. "Good for you," he said eventually. "Remind me to keep my manners in place around you." His smile was reassuring.

Lina didn't expect that reaction, and therefore didn't trust it. Maybe he only said what he assumed she wanted to hear. She'd have to keep an eye on him, which was not a hardship. "I need to get back to my apartment, but now I'm afraid to go there."

"Don't be. I'll protect you."

"Why? I thought you were working for my parents."

"In theory I am simply 'looking into the preliminary case' so far, but again, they never wanted me to search in Las Vegas. I'm fairly certain they fired several other agencies for even suggesting it. I was doing a little personal research before deciding whether to take the case."

"Why did you come to Las Vegas, then?"

He shook his head. "I didn't. I was already here."

Lina studied him for a moment, searching his gorgeous face for the truth. His features were not the sharply angled countenance of the man who'd grabbed her.

Dalton was a tall, blue-eyed, blond-haired all-American boy type. His face was beautiful, especially when he smiled. A stronger sense of recognition brushed her memory again. He looked amazingly like the man who'd come into the Big Tent Buffet when she'd started working at the Carnival Club Casino, making her first week very exciting. She'd been jumpy, sure someone would recognize her and drag her back to Arizona, so she'd kept her head down when he'd briefly talked to her.

The very tall man, possibly Dalton, had chased a guy out of the buffet, into the main casino and out of the hotel. She found out later that the police had charged the subject of the chase for some previous crime. She'd looked for the tall man in the restaurant later on, but hadn't seen him again. Was this him?

"What are your intentions?" she asked, trying not to sound as wary as she felt.

"Well, first off, I'd like to ensure your safety. I'm happy to protect you and get you back to your apartment."

"Why would you do that for me?"

"In my opinion, strange men shouldn't go around grabbing women without their permission. Whoever he was, he got what he deserved. I'll dish out more and worse if he's still there or tries anything else with you." He glanced at the three men littering the ground around them. "Besides, I do owe you for helping me. And I'll be prepared next time for them to play dirty."

"Okay. Then what? Obviously, I can't stay at my apartment any longer. If you and that awful stranger found me, others will, too."

"I have a vehicle. I could take you to a motel—"

"I can barely afford my apartment with four other girls. I don't have money for a motel." *Not yet anyway. And I can't trust you, can I?*

Her tone came out sounding mean, but she was mostly frustrated. If she had to leave Las Vegas and start all over somewhere else, she'd be heartbroken. Not that she wouldn't do it, but how soul-wrenching to have to start over.

She crossed her arms, checking over her shoulder every few seconds to see if the man who'd assaulted her was up and about and ready to take revenge on her.

Looking at Dalton didn't help. Staring at him put her romantic frame of mind into a tailspin. It was disconcerting to have such lustful thoughts about this man—the hired gun her parents sent to find her. She wasn't certain what he'd do in the long run. Or the short run, for that matter. She needed help, but she absolutely could not trust him.

"How about I take you somewhere to eat? We can talk about what you want to do over a nice meal."

"I do not believe our interests are aligned," she said,

trying not to sound bitchy or, worse, flirty. "Obviously, I don't want my parents to know I'm here."

He inhaled deeply. "I don't have to report anything...yet."

"Yet?"

"Hear me out. I only agreed to look into this case at all because I'm a sucker for parents looking for missing children."

"I'm not a child." She straightened to her full unimpressive height, looking up into his slightly battered face. "I'm over twenty-one. I can do as I please."

"Yes. That is true. Also I was told specifically that I would not find you in Las Vegas and not to even bother looking here. They wanted me to go to New York and start there."

Lina shook her head. "I knew they would never think I'd dare come here."

"I could call and tell them I'd like to look around here in Las Vegas—"

"Waste of time," Lina said under her breath.

"—and see if I can get fired."

CHAPTER 6

"What? Why would you do that?" she asked Dalton, with earnest eyes in a color he wasn't expecting. He thought her eyes would be dark, exotic, but they were sort of a gray blue. In fact, the two of them shared the same hair color and eye color.

Dalton responded slowly and carefully to her question. "I guess even more than missing daughters, I don't like to see women without choices. You *are* over twenty-one. You should be able to do whatever you want to, within reason and the law.

"Besides, I was on vacation. Like I said, I only looked into the case initially because of what turned out to be slight misinformation. Also, if they've hired someone else, I don't need to be involved." He looked down at the men still decorating the sidewalk, grateful no one had discovered them yet.

She stared at him for a long time before nodding. "Thank you."

"My pleasure. What would you like to do?" Dalton sidestepped the three men he'd tangled with, wondering if her parents had called in another agency. Maybe he'd fire them first.

He'd only agreed to look into the job because they

seemed desperate and out of options. If they had engaged other agencies, the tentative agreement he'd made with them was null and void. It wasn't a hardship to change to her side at this early juncture.

"If you would please escort me, I'd like to go back to my apartment and retrieve my things. Then I need to go somewhere unexpected, where no one would think to look for me. I'm not sure where that is yet."

He nodded. "Lead the way. We'll figure it all out as we go."

One of the men started to stir as they hurried away. A car passed by, but didn't stop or even slow down to investigate the three men on the ground. He didn't like to think of Lina living in the kind of neighborhood where bodies on the ground weren't worth a second glance.

When they got to the hedge-lined walkway, she allowed him to take the lead, but stayed within arm's length as they continued forward. Dalton let her trail behind him, keeping a wary eye out for a possible attack.

Rounding the corner to the short sidewalk leading to her apartment, Dalton scanned the area. It was deserted. Halfway down, the foliage of the hedge on the left side was crushed. Leaves and small twigs littered the walkway.

Lina pointed. "That's where he pinned me."

Dalton put his arm around her shoulders, offering comfort, and hoped she wouldn't shy away. She moved closer, snuggling her head against his chest as they walked to her door. His heart sped up like some lovesick idiot the moment she engaged, but he ignored it, trying to be noble and gallant.

She opened her door with a key and entered, motioning for him to follow. He closed the door behind him, turning toward the chaos of the loud apartment.

The television was on and the volume seemed to be

set at ear-piercing. The lingering smell of burnt toast hung in the air and the roommate he'd talked to was kicked back on the sofa, head bent over her phone, thumb typing at an impressive speed.

"Chrissy," Lina said. "Did anyone else come to the door after I left?"

"What?" The girl asked, taking distracted to a whole new level. Her thumbs never slowed. Lina moved closer to the sofa. The girl stopped typing all of a sudden and promptly held the phone away from Lina, out of reach, her expression defiant as she stared at her roommate.

Lina returned the same rebellious look and said, "Did anyone else come to the door after I went to the library?"

Chrissy glanced at Dalton, still parked by the front door. "No. No one else came here, just him. I see you found each other." Chrissy's phone made a jangling noise and she pulled the device close to her chest, turning halfway toward the sofa as if fearful someone was about to snatch it out of her hands. Her furious tapping resumed.

Lina glanced over her shoulder at him, rolling her eyes. He grinned. Perhaps Chrissy was right to be afraid. In the same position, that's exactly what he would have done.

Lina wasn't someone active in social media even before she left home for Las Vegas. Any presence afterward, weak or strong, was giving everyone in the world the option of finding her. It was rather impressive how she'd remained out of sight for all these months, although changing her appearance had likely helped.

He was impressed. Every moment he spent in her presence made him like her even more. She didn't come across as rich, spoiled or coddled. Instead, she was smart, motivated and hard-working.

Dalton was definitely leaning in the direction of dumping her parents' offer and aligning with Lina.

Maybe he'd invite her along on his spontaneous vacation. Certainly no one would find them, as he didn't have a specific itinerary in mind. Wouldn't it be fun to have someone to share his time off with? Dalton shook his head, as if that would help dislodge his foolish infatuation with a strong, clever woman facing possibly difficult choices.

Lina reached toward him, waving her fingers and signaling him to follow her. She walked past the blaring television, down a short hallway to a door on the left. Knocking twice, she entered a moment later.

Dalton followed her inside a fairly neat, if crowded room. There were two twin beds, between them a nightstand with a small lamp centered on it, a bench-seat trunk at the foot of each bed and a large dresser against the wall that barely cleared the swing of the bedroom door.

Lina went to the closet and slid open one side of a mirrored door. Inside, it wasn't full by half. She grabbed a backpack off the shelf above the rod. Was it the one she'd carried from Flagstaff?

Tossing her pack on the nearest bed, she opened the top flap and started stuffing things from the closet inside with a quick fold-and-shove method he admired.

"Can I help?" he asked to be polite, not totally opposed to the idea of helping grab her underclothes out of her dresser, if that would be useful.

"No. Thanks. I'll just be a minute." She turned and disappeared into the adjoining bathroom. He heard some rustling around in a cabinet. She returned with a yellow-topped aerosol can of bathroom cleaner and shoved it inside her bag. She caught him watching her. They stared at one another for what felt like a solid ten seconds.

The more he stared the more he wanted to take her in his arms and discover what she tasted like. He looked away first, wondering what in the hell he was thinking. Dalton was never so impacted by watching a woman pack her things. What was wrong with him?

When he mastered some control over his feelings, he chanced another look in her direction. She'd moved on to her dresser, pulling the second drawer from the top out halfway. She reached inside and scooped out a pile of colorful underthings. Without looking at him, she stuck the whole mass of skimpy fabric into the backpack.

He was grateful, as his current expression might border on unsuitable. Mentally, he scolded himself for his lack of control. She pulled another drawer open and grabbed up several folded pairs of dark socks.

Back at her closet again, she pulled out three pairs of jeans, folded them haphazardly and stuffed them into the now-bulging bag. Several shirts also went in along with a pair of strappy sandals. As the visual of her dainty feet encased in the scanty footwear threatened to reveal his attraction, Dalton cleared his throat and forced himself to look away.

She didn't seem to notice his struggle to maintain his calm in her enticing presence. Another quick trip into the bathroom for a small zippered makeup bag. It was the last thing she put in her backpack before pulling the string tie closed, flipping the top flap in place and securing it with a snap.

Dalton picked her bag up and slung it over one shoulder. She smiled and turned back to her closet. From deep within she pulled a garment bag out and folded it over one arm. A smallish carpetbag was also pulled out and settled in the hand with the garment bag.

"I'm ready to go," she said.

"That's the fastest I've ever seen a girl pack up all her things in my life." He hoped she didn't notice his growing interest.

"Thank you. I think."

Dalton looked down at her, admiring her beautiful blue eyes. The color was so unexpected. "Where can I take you?"

Her gaze turned upward in return, zeroing in on his face. "I was hoping we could go to your hotel room."

"I beg your pardon. *My* hotel room?" The shocked look in Dalton's eyes and his mouth dropping open amused her, but she tried not to show it.

"Yes. You say you work alone. I don't know who else is after me. Neither do you. Who would look for me at your place?" She stared at him again. "Unless you told my parents where you were staying. Did you?"

"No. I didn't share my hotel information with a client." His tone was not sarcastic, but perhaps edging that way.

"I didn't mean any insult, just explaining my thinking."

He relaxed and one of his shoulders lifted in a half-shrug. "No worries. You make a good point."

"Also, I have to trust you *not* to reveal my location to my parents. Is that still your goal?"

"If they've hired someone else, it makes any initial contract I had with them void anyway."

She studied him again. He looked like he wanted to help her. It seemed like he didn't want to help her parents, since they hadn't been forthcoming about their objectives and had steered him away from where he'd actually found her.

"Is it your intention to help me?" They'd be all alone in his hotel room. Why did that give her a thrill?

Dalton cleared his throat, as if suddenly uncomfortable.

"Yes. I'll help you."

"And you won't contact my parents or at least not until I'm safely out of their reach again, yes?"

He smiled. "Yes. Until you're safe."

He could change his mind. His connection with her parents could still be problematic for her later, but he was literally her only hope right now. Either that or she'd have to run on her own. That was still an option if Dalton proved untrustworthy. She had a good feeling about him, though. He could help her in the short term.

"Then we're good, yes?"

He smiled that gorgeous smile and said, "Yes. We're good. Let's go."

Lina was operating on only the barest level of trust, but Dalton seemed honorable.

The man pretending to be Dalton was more troublesome. He'd mentioned she should go back for her duty and *that* sounded more like someone sent by her parents. He was the main reason she'd decided to trust Dalton.

Dalton didn't say the word *duty*, nor did he frighten her like the other man had. His impact was quite the opposite. He soothed her frayed nerves as much as he intrigued her. She shouldn't think about him in a romantic light, but she couldn't seem to help it.

Lina left her shared bedroom, crossed the hall and knocked on the other door. No one answered. She opened it, stuck her head inside and then opened the door wider.

This room also had two twin beds, but that was where the similarity ended. It was a disaster area.

Dalton whispered, "Wait. I'm afraid to walk in here. There are clothes and shoes and all manner of girly things littered on the floor."

Lina looked down. Not a single bit of cheap carpet showed through the mess. She walked without hesitation across the littered floor to the window between the two twin beds without regard to the horrid way her roommates kept their shared space.

"They won't notice, trust me. A herd of buffalo could stampede through here without being noticed." Dalton looked dubious, but smiled at her comment and followed her.

She opened the window easily, stuck her head out and looked around. She then carefully placed her garment bag and small carpetbag outside. One boot-covered foot went straight out the open window. She then scrunched down, folding her body through the opening and finally pulled her other leg out.

"I'm not sure I'll fit through here," he said once she was outside.

"You can make it."

He pushed her backpack through the opening and carefully stuck his leg through, ducking down to get his body flat. It looked like he scraped his entire spine along the bottom edge of the window, but he made it through and didn't complain about sneaking out this way. She was grateful.

"See. No problem," she said by way of reassurance. He smiled and slung the backpack over one shoulder. She grabbed his hand. The feel of his strong, callused palm in hers sent a spasm of intensity from their connection to her lovesick heart. "Which way to your vehicle?" she asked in a low tone.

Dalton squeezed her fingers and led the way around the back side of her apartment complex to a side street. He popped the back hatch of a large, black SUV with Arizona tags. They quickly dumped all her things in the back compartment and hopped into the front seat before seeing anyone on the road.

He started the SUV and they were away in no time. The dark tint of the windows made her feel completely concealed for maybe the first time since she'd arrived in Las Vegas.

Glancing into the side mirror, she watched to see if anyone followed.

"No one is behind us," he said, adding in an amused tone, "I think we made a clean getaway."

"You are making fun of me."

"No." He paused and shot her a quick amused look. "Okay, maybe a little. You take this cloak and dagger stuff very seriously."

"If you were in my position, you'd do the same thing."

"Maybe I would. However, I'm not certain exactly what your position is. I don't know why your parents wanted me to find you. Would you be willing to share a little bit of your story?"

"My parents arranged a marriage for me."

"Ah. And you didn't want to marry the man they'd chosen?"

"Not really, but I did it anyway. I married him."

"You're married!" He couldn't have sounded or looked more dismayed.

Lina shook her head. "No. He died. So now I'm a widow."

His voice softened. "Oh. I'm sorry."

"Don't be. It was a very short marriage." *Less than one day, in fact.*

"Why did you leave home?"

"My parents then began negotiations for a second arranged marriage. And I didn't want any part of it. They insisted it was my duty, but they already promised that if I went through with the first marriage—and my husband got his citizenship—they'd allow a quiet divorce and let me have modest funds to live my life as I chose."

"Huh." Dalton narrowed his brows. "Not to be judgy or anything, but isn't that illegal?"

A dark laugh exited before she could stop it. "Do you not know the name Dragovic?" *They do as they wish, skirting the law as it suits them. Everyone knows that.*

He nodded, as if that explained everything. "I've heard some things. I couldn't say what is the truth or what are lies meant to add drama and mystique."

"Making fun again?"

One shoulder lifted and dropped. "No. I'm not making fun so much as I'm surprised at how thoughtful you are about the decisions you've made, given your challenges. I'm also impressed. I like smart women."

"Thank you." Lina melted a little bit more at his sincere compliment. She caught glances of his handsome profile as he drove. She so wanted him to be the honorable guy she needed.

He took them toward Las Vegas Boulevard and the main strip, where many of the larger hotels were. Lina considered again where she might have seen Dalton. Did he ever stay at the Carnival Club Casino? Was that why he looked familiar? Is that where they were headed right now?

She glanced in his direction again. "What hotel are you staying at here in town?"

"The Blue Diamond."

Her relief must have shown because he asked, "Is that good news?"

She shrugged, trying to look nonchalant. The Blue Diamond *was* the hotel nearest to the Carnival Club Casino, but still quite a ways apart, thanks to the large empty lot between the two casinos. One of the older hotels had been brought down last year and new construction had been delayed due to an unresolved dispute between the builder and the developer.

"Were you afraid I'd say the Carnival Club Casino?"

"No," she lied.

"I know that's where you work. I have stayed there in the past. The last time was three months ago when I chased a guy out of the hotel. Maybe that's why you look familiar to me. Did you work there then?" He watched her closely. So they both found each other familiar. Interesting.

"I started working there about three months ago."

"Do you remember the guy who ran out of the hotel's buffet and out of the hotel onto the street chasing a criminal? That was me."

"Maybe," she said, but she was shocked again. They *had* met before. He'd come into the restaurant as she'd been leaving. He had flashed a photo in her direction of a guy she'd seen inside the restaurant, asking briskly, "Have you seen this guy?"

Lina had studied the photo, nodded and pointed in the direction of the man's booth. Dalton had mumbled a quick, "Thank you," and raced toward the booth. The man had leapt up and Dalton promptly chased after him. She'd only briefly seen Dalton's face, his eyes and...well, his backside as he'd run after his prey. She remembered that fondly.

Dalton drove to the rear entrance of the Blue Diamond, away from the main strip. He parked near the elevators on the fourth floor of a seven-story parking structure attached to the hotel.

He took her things from the trunk, not letting her carry any of it. They got on the elevator and he pushed the button for the fifteenth floor. They stepped off the elevator and headed to his room.

Once inside the spacious entry, the door closed behind her, Lina relaxed for the first time since leaving her apartment through her roommates' window.

She walked down a short hall and into the plush room. A king-size bed took up most of the right side of the room.

Her calm disappeared and a new worry came to mind. Of course he would have only one bed.

The question was, would he expect to share it with her?

She'd been insistent on coming to his hotel room. What might he expect in return? What price might she have to pay in order to remain? Lina looked at him over one shoulder.

Did he think she wanted him? Because she *did* want him. Did he want *her*? Did he want her enough to keep quiet about her whereabouts? Maybe she didn't care if it meant she got a chance to spend some intimate time with him.

She shook off her growing lust and scanned the luxurious room.

Dalton placed her things in the closet by the door, including her precious backpack, the only thing she'd brought to Las Vegas with her.

"Are you hungry?" he asked, without looking in her direction. "I could order some room service for us. I haven't eaten yet."

Her stomach flipped over at the mere suggestion of food. The meal she'd had a couple of hours ago at work had been filling. After the stress of the evening, it was a wonder she hadn't acquired a stomachache.

"No, thanks. You go ahead, though."

"Are you really going to make me eat alone and in front of you?" His gaze searched her out, pinning her with a question in his storm-colored eyes.

She smiled. "I had a big dinner earlier, but I'll have coffee and dessert. Will that work?"

"Yes. Perfect. What sweet treat would you like to have?"

"I don't care. Surprise me." She moved from the foot of the bed over to the window, where a sliding glass door led to a small terrace. She opened the door, letting in the breeze, stepped outside, seated herself on one of the chairs and looked out at the view of the city. For some reason, it felt more hidden out here.

Maybe it was because Dalton filled the room so very well with his tall, virile presence and irresistible masculine scent. Lina would have to keep her guard up around him. He could easily seduce her into trying wicked things she'd never been interested in with anyone else.

Before going down that seductive path, perhaps she should assess what he was after. She hadn't cataloged him quite yet, fast-made friend or future foe. Possibly both titles fit him.

A slice of memory intruded. She pictured Dalton running after the man in the hotel. She remembered the determined look on his face, the incredible speed as he ran after the man he sought. He was serious about getting his man. Was he the same way about getting his woman? Time would tell.

If he became her foe, would he chase after her with the same relentless intensity? Undoubtedly. He'd certainly catch her without much effort. In the meantime, should she allow herself the luxury of temptation? Every time she stared at him, he made her insides feel melty, happy and safe. Should she trust him in the short term until he disappointed her by fulfilling her parents' wishes, hauling her back to face an unwanted second arranged marriage?

Did she want to be tempted?

A quick look over her shoulder was timed perfectly. Dalton finished his call for room service and hung up. He suddenly peeled his mussed and torn shirt off, gifting her with a great eyeful of his bare, beautiful, muscular upper half, and giving her the answer she'd sought earlier.

That would be a big, fat *yes* in the temptation department.

CHAPTER 7

Dalton ordered a burger and fries from room service and also a piece of chocolate cake and a slice of cherry pie, wanting to offer her a choice. His shirt was a mess from the fight so he pulled it off and grabbed a T-shirt as a replacement, then cleaned up his face in the bathroom.

Once he was a bit more presentable, he joined her on the small terrace until the food arrived.

She looked lovely, seated quietly on his private terrace as if she didn't have a care in the world. A slight breeze ruffled her hair, taking his thoughts back to that photo in the bus station. "I liked your long dark hair and the ponytail in the bus station photo," he said before realizing he planned to say anything out loud. "But I have to say I love the cut and color now even more."

She smiled, seemingly surprised by his compliment. "Thank you. This is actually my natural color."

"Is it?"

She nodded. "I dyed it regularly starting a long time ago. No one ever believed I belonged to my parents, who both have dark hair. But my granny had blond hair in her youth. So I come by it honestly."

"No doubt."

"Did you say you were on vacation?"

"Yes."

"Lucky you. I'd love a vacation. But I can't afford any extended time away from my job."

"Why not?"

She pushed out a deep sigh. "I was about to say I had a financial goal to reach, but I think my plans have been changed for me. I'm not certain what I'll do next."

"You're welcome to stay with me as long as you want," Dalton said off-handedly. Having a target stay with him was problematic on so many levels of his complicated life he wondered at his stupidity in offering.

"I don't really know you well enough to do that."

Dalton narrowed his gaze when she turned him down. He felt like a sullen child being told he had to stop playing and come inside to eat dinner. *What the fuck is wrong with me?*

"No offense intended," she said quickly, seeing his scowl.

He forced himself to unclench and smile. "None taken. I haven't had any time off in a while. I may have forgotten how to relax at all."

Her smile was quick and she laughed. Extraordinary. "You are forgiven," she said, and stared at his mouth for several seconds, making the blood in his veins heat up. He let her stare. Speaking would break the mood. He lowered his gaze to her mouth, too. Truly extraordinary.

Lina shook her head slightly and the sultry moment was broken. She turned her head to stare out at the lights of the city.

Dalton remained quiet for a few minutes, enjoying the silent, beautiful company.

"Will you spend your entire vacation in Las Vegas?" she asked quietly.

"No. I like to move around."

Her head spun back to stare at him again. "What do you mean, move around?"

He shrugged. "I was only going to be here for a few days before moving on to someplace else."

"Where will you go next?"

"Not sure yet. Lake Havasu, maybe."

"Really?" Her expression brightened. "I'd love to go there."

"I have a small RV there parked near the lake."

"Is it on private land?"

"No. I thought putting it in the Coyote Willow campground would lend it more of a hiding-in-plain-sight feel rather than putting it on private land that would have to be wired with cameras, sensors and then guarded all the time to ensure security."

She nodded, seeming to get it. "Do you also have a boat?"

"Nope. I rent them as it suits me. My job doesn't lend itself to settling down, as a rule. I prefer being able to make quick getaways. After Lake Havasu, I'm not sure where I'll go. I like to be spontaneous with my time off."

"I'd imagine a security specialist could spend a lot of time on the road. I'm surprised you don't want to rest up in one place."

"Actually, I've always been more of a bounty hunter than a security specialist. Maybe the rootless existence suits me even when I vacation."

"Bounty hunter? Is that why my parents hired you?" Her alarm was evident.

"I do have a reputation for being able to find people consistently."

"You certainly hunted me down fast enough."

He shrugged. "Only because lots of legwork had already been done by other agencies your parents hired. They left behind great notes. The truth is, I got lucky."

"Are you sure you won't turn me in? Is there a high price or a bounty on my head?"

A knock at the door kept him from having to answer her question.

"That's the food. I'll be right back. Want to eat out here?"

She looked wary for a second, then nodded. "Out here is fine."

"I hope you like the surprise dessert I ordered." His gaze rested on her face for longer than a few seconds. He'd rather talk about dessert and what might happen after she'd eaten it than his barely defined arrangement with her parents.

There *was* a substantial bounty involved in her discovery and more for her return. Dalton had never worked cheap. In this case, he didn't want to tell her the sizable sum her parents had put up for her return and hoped she didn't find out. She might not trust him with the generous value of the bounty involved.

And Dalton wanted her trust.

The size of the bounty meant if *he* didn't bring her in, someone else certainly would try to. This was new ground for him, serving as a protector and guardian to someone on the run instead of taking his standard pursuer-and-predator approach to hunting people down.

If he ever decided to hunt Lina, the reason would involve pure primal intent with a side of animal instinct in order to persuade her to spend quality alone time with him. He'd have to devote more effort to ensure she knew she could trust him.

Protecting her with the intent of keeping her became a new thought running roughshod over any business concerns to find her and return her to her parents. She was unique and he was smart enough to know it.

"I'm certain I will like whatever you chose." Lina wished for things that she shouldn't want. His intense stare was fiercely possessive. Worse, she liked it.

When another, harder knock sounded, Dalton broke their heated gaze and left to answer the door.

Lina was on dangerous ground. Sensual electricity arced between them each second they spent together. She wanted to explore the longing she had for this intriguing man. It was the first time she'd ever felt so strongly attracted to anyone. She'd probably already be in bed with him if he hadn't told her why he'd looked her up. He hadn't made any overt statements of keeping her safe forever.

She wasn't sure if she could trust him. Not yet. She didn't want to go back to her parents. She most assuredly didn't want to go back as Dalton's valuable bounty after being hunted down. Was that still any part of his intention?

Yes, he'd helped her. They were in his hotel hiding out.

Yes, he was very attractive. She'd never been so tempted by a pretty face before.

Yes, she wanted to do wild, wicked things on that king-size bed. When would she ever get another chance like this?

Could she trust him in the short term to satisfy her curiosity about her volatile attraction?

No. She shouldn't get involved or allow anything to happen between them. She was on the run from an arranged marriage and her parents wanted him to hunt her down, bring her home and make her pay for the audacity of leaving.

Lina needed to keep that fact at the forefront of her mind whenever her libido gave its opinion. Another quick look in his direction melted her resolve to part from him anytime soon. She was weak for him.

A lanky young waiter in a nice white jacket rolled the cart to the terrace and placed the dishes on the outdoor table as Dalton signed the check. The waiter thanked

Dalton, smiled cordially at her, and exited the room.

Dalton had saved her, hidden her and was now feeding her.

What might he want in payment to remain on her side against her parents? Unclear. What did she want to give him? Everything.

What would it hurt if she took tonight to fulfill a wild dream, throwing caution to the wind instead of worrying about every single blessed thing? Possibly a lot. But it didn't lessen her desire for the freedom this one single night might offer.

Dalton pointed to the table sporting not one but two luscious-looking desserts. "Chocolate cake or cherry pie. Which one do you want?" His gaze looked wanton, for lack of a better word. Her libido surged to the forefront to make its opinion clear. *I want you.*

"Too hard to choose," she managed to respond. "How about we share them? Then we get a taste of each treat."

He grinned again his most perfect smile. She was lost to it. She wanted him. "Great idea," his low-toned response went all the way to her bones in vibrant reaction.

Dalton ate his burger and fries quickly and efficiently. She stole several fries from his plate as she sipped her coffee, but he'd offered.

They split the desserts and then watched each other eat bite after bite of sweet chocolate fudge layer cake and tart cherry pie.

"I don't know which one I like better," he said, finishing the last forkful of cake as he stared at her mouth.

"They were both very good." Lina stared back at his beautiful eyes with equal intensity.

What would happen if she let her guard down for one single night? It was ludicrous to believe she didn't know the exact answer to that question. She knew.

Lina would be swallowed up with desire and would finally know what it meant to have sex with an attractive man. She'd thought about it more than once throughout their short time together. Ultimately, she didn't want to give up this opportunity. As a widowed virgin, Lina had thought quite a lot about sex in the months before and after leaving home.

If she'd stayed and been married off to the other Zupan son, it might have been her first initiation into sexual experience, since the families wanted an heir. But she didn't know what either of the Zupan men looked like or if they were nice or mean or elitist or of the privileged class looking down their noses at working people like she'd become in her journey away from home.

Even though it was difficult, Lina derived a sense of satisfaction from working and earning money to live life on her terms.

She wanted to know what it was to be intimate with a man. Lina, however, wanted a man of *her* choosing and not her parents' selection based on financial gain.

He saw her glance toward the huge bed. Now he had to know what was in her head, as well.

The music he'd put on after answering the door suddenly seemed louder out on the terrace. The strains of a classic romantic ballad started up, filling the air with notes and words meant to enflame and nudge and lure her into even more wickedly lustful thoughts.

"Dance with me," he said and stood up, offering her a hand.

She should have turned him down. She should have said no thank you. Lina put her small hand in his big palm. He led her into the room, near the bed. Not hard to do, as the bed took up the majority of the space. That fact rolled around in her head as he loosely took her in his arms.

As she'd guessed, the top of her head barely reached his shoulders. Lina pressed her face into his chest. The sound of his heartbeat was solid and strong and secure. She relaxed into him, cataloguing every place they touched.

Her right palm pressed into his left one. Her left rested on his shoulder. His other hand was firmly secured in the center of her spine, pressing lightly with every step as if he wanted her even closer. She obliged and he led her slowly around the open space at the end of the bed.

He leaned his head down, brushing his face on the top of her head in a gesture so caring, she was lost to him. She'd do anything with him or for him in this sultry moment. She wanted him, soon. No, now.

The last note of the song faded and a more upbeat song started. Lina stepped back, tilting her head up to stare into his eyes, wanting to make her desires known.

Dalton inhaled half a breath as she pulled away and looked into her eyes. She saw the faintest smile, of triumph, perhaps, or relief. Without commenting or looking away, he sat down on the end of the bed and pulled her between his open legs.

This put her in the superior position of looking down at him. No man in the world she'd run from would ever do such a thing. She felt all-powerful as he drew her closer. His firm embrace encompassed her body and soul. His willingness to let her lead filled her with passion and joy and lust. She lowered her mouth and kissed him hard, opening her lips against his for a first taste.

He saw her coming, but seemed tentative in opening to her, as if giving her a chance to change her mind. She was not going to change her mind. She wanted many things in her life, chief among them the freedom to do as she pleased. But in this particular moment she wanted Dalton Langston, Security Specialist, with an intense desire she'd never felt before.

She moaned as the flavor of cherry and chocolate registered. His tongue licked slowly and purposefully inside her mouth, tangling, stroking, tasting and seducing her with each subtle movement.

Lina was lost to his kiss and ready for a spontaneous and unexpected night of passion in the arms of a stranger. Her heart nearly exploded with the seductive possibilities.

Inhaling his intoxicating masculine scent as their kiss escalated made her soul dance in pleasure. Clutched in his strong grasp, Lina relaxed, melding her body into him, pressing him back down on the bed.

He made her feel safe. He made her feel wanted. He made her feel like all things were possible if only she trusted him. She let go of any lingering inhibitions and pressed forward to explore this seductive dance of love, hoping she'd come away with a memorable experience at the very least. She only wanted one night to herself. She deserved it.

Lina kissed him harder, licking her tongue between his firm, smooth lips. Suddenly, he was no longer tentative. Seconds later, he proceeded to devour her. She liked it.

His arms tightened around her body. He twisted her onto her back on the bed next to him, half covering her with his torso, as if he needed to do so to be able to kiss her harder and more thoroughly.

She was undone. She was ready for anything. She wanted him now.

His phone vibrated in his pocket, breaking them apart in surprise. He released a deep, long breath, pulled one hand away from her and reached inside his pocket for his cellular.

"Sorry," he whispered.

At first he glanced at the screen like he was about to shut it off or toss it over one shoulder, but then his eyes narrowed, and he answered the call instead.

"Yes," he said rather curtly into the phone. Seconds later, he darted a quick look to her face. He put his finger up, signaling either that he needed a minute or to wait.

In the space of two more seconds, he eased away from her carefully. "Yes," he said again, his gaze lighting guiltily on her for only a moment before he completely removed himself from the bed, stood up and left her immediate space. She was bereft in his absence, and felt foolish for wanting what she was obviously not going to get.

Dalton closed the bathroom door, silencing any further comments he made to the mysterious caller, leaving her thoroughly kissed, but unsatisfied as to further lovemaking possibilities.

Had he come to his senses? Would he initiate another kiss upon his return? She hoped so, but worried that wasn't going to happen as the minutes ticked by. The more time he spent away, the more likely it was they would not resume the volatile kiss, leading to whatever might happen on his huge bed.

If that was the way he kissed, she might not make it through the expressive passion of his lovemaking. She did know she wanted to give her best effort. Maybe she should undress and wait for him in bed.

Lina only had time to untuck her T-shirt from her jeans before Dalton exited the bathroom. He returned to the side of the bed.

"That was your parents," he said, looking rather miserable.

"What?" She sat up straight, no longer languid. "What did you tell them?"

"I told them I wanted to start in Las Vegas since I

was already here. I expected them to fire me on the spot."

"Did they?" Lina hoped against hope that they had.

"No. They already wired a down payment into my account. I'm supposed to start in earnest as soon as possible. I told them first thing tomorrow morning."

CHAPTER 8

"Tomorrow morning?" Lina scrambled off the bed as if ready to bolt from the room, from the hotel and from this city in the next few seconds.

Dalton reached for her. He expected her to push him away, but she didn't. The moment his arms wound around her tiny frame, she attached herself to him.

"I'm sorry," he said, squeezing her tight, kissing her forehead, until she tilted her face toward his. Her look was frightened but trusting. She shouldn't trust him. He hadn't told her the worst part yet. He didn't want to tell her. He was already obligated not to tell her.

Dalton wasn't certain about the order of events, but seconds later, she was kissing him like they were about to be parted forever and guiding him back to his bed. Soon they'd resumed the hot kiss the call had interrupted.

He let himself go, kissing her like he wanted to, pressing her into the mattress of his large bed, wondering how he'd be able to reconcile his contracted debt to her parents and still keep her safe. Or rather, keep her to himself.

Dalton had been surprised by her hot, aggressive kiss after they finished dessert. He'd been passive for the first few seconds, partly trying to get over the shock of her doing the one thing he'd been thinking about since they entered his hotel room.

Once she deepened their first kiss, he gave as good as he got. The unique attachment he felt for her grew stronger with each passing moment, until his phone buzzed in his pocket. He'd been about to throw it across the room, but saw the name Dragovic on the screen.

He'd only communicated with her parents by e-mail. The phone call meant he'd basically gotten caught with his pants down in a wholly compromising position with the girl he was supposed to be finding for her worried parents. He'd practically barked the word, "Yes," into the phone, hating to be distracted from Lina and her sexy kisses.

"This is Ivan Dragovic. I am speaking with Dalton Langston, yes?"

"Yes," Dalton had said as calmly as his racing heart would allow as he extricated himself from Lina's warm, tempting body.

"I want to finalize our arrangement," her father said.

"About that," Dalton said in a low tone, closing the bathroom door. "I may not be able to help you with this assignment." *I refuse to help you marry Lina off to another rich foreign loser trying to gain citizenship illegally.*

"You come highly recommended by many associates of mine. Only you can help me."

Dalton searched his brain for a good enough excuse to reject his offer. "I've recently started a long-anticipated vacation." *Totally lame.*

"I'll pay you double your standard fee to start tomorrow morning," the man said in a deep and lightly accented, assertive tone. It was likely Kzeratian, which sounded very similar to Russian to Dalton's ear.

"Tomorrow morning?" Dalton ran his hand over the

top of his head, scraping his fingernails along his scalp, thinking furiously to find a way out of this job. He faced the wall, the only thing separating him from Lina.

He would not admit that he'd already found her. Not yet. He hadn't absolutely agreed to take the job. He didn't want it. He especially didn't want to be the one to bring her to heel and hand her over to her parents like she was some criminal. He should drop this before it got started.

Before Dalton could say another word, Ivan Dragovic said, "I've already wired the first half of the standard fee to your account. I'll wire the balance when the bank opens in the morning."

Fuck. What to do now? Fuck.

"Fine," he said rather crossly. "I will postpone my vacation starting tomorrow morning after I see the deposit. What is it that you expect, Mr. Dragovic?"

"What is your meaning?"

"Your daughter is an adult. If I find her, what is it that you expect me to do? Legally, the best I can do is to ask her to go home and then escort her there if she agrees. I don't have the authority to take her into custody if she doesn't wish to come."

"That will be no problem. I have sworn out a warrant for her arrest and informed the authorities that I have a private consultant, or rather you, searching for her."

"What?"

"As a registered bounty hunter you have full authority to bring her back for her arraignment in Arizona, regardless of what state she is in as stipulated by the charges against her."

"Charges?" Dalton asked, acid swirling violently in his belly. "What are the charges against her?"

"Felony theft of very valuable family jewelry. Naturally we want this kept out of the public eye."

Naturally.

Dalton wasn't certain this method was a hundred percent legal, but Ivan Dragovic likely operated under his own authority.

"She's a thief?" Dalton asked incredulously. It was the only non-volatile thing he could think to say rather than what he wanted to scream, which included, "What kind of horrible father puts a dubious felony charge against his own daughter?"

Dragovic didn't say anything for a few silent seconds. "That is the charge leveled against her and one that you can use to bring her back home. It's a means to an end. Home is where Nikolina belongs. We know what's best for her."

Ah. Dalton took the last statement to mean Lina was probably innocent of the charges, but her family was playing hardball to get her to return. He wondered why. He didn't think it was because they missed her or loved her so much they had to have her back. There had been more than one whispered conversation in Ironwood about the Dragovic family and how they operated.

Lina moaned a sultry sound of desire against his lips and Dalton reeled quickly back into the present.

"Lina," he said, wanting to continue, but afraid to go too far, considering the uncertainty and scope of his obligation.

"Dalton," she whispered. "Please don't stop." Her sweet breath brushed against one cheek.

He pulled away enough to see her swollen, kiss-moistened lips, wanting nothing more than to bury himself into her repeatedly for the rest of the night, but unsure she'd be willing when she learned about his job. The one he'd unwillingly committed to—because of the wired payment—starting tomorrow morning.

"I don't want to stop," he said.

Before he could say more, she kissed him quickly. "We have until tomorrow morning, yes?"

Dalton stared down into her beautiful face. "Technically, yes."

"Then let's take advantage of our limited time together. No one is looking for me tonight. I'm free for now and I want you. I wish to be spontaneous one last time. Will you please let me have this one night with you, just the two of us together all night long?"

He couldn't argue with her logic and wanted her too much to turn her away. "Yes, one night with just the two of us. I will gladly and gratefully do that for us both."

Dalton kissed her with singular focus and forgot about absolutely everything else with the exception of the gorgeous woman in his arms, seeking spontaneity with him for this one glorious night.

Lina was awash in sensual pleasure so intense, she forgot about pretty much everything else. Dalton kissed her like she was the only woman in the world who mattered.

Without speaking, he pulled her from the surface of the bed. In between luscious lip-locks, they undressed each other.

Once their T-shirts, jeans, shoes and underthings were scattered on the floor, Dalton pulled the sheets down and pressed her into his huge bed. Naked and aroused, he was spectacular to look at and even more overwhelming pressed to her naked body, sending her untried feelings of love straight into overdrive.

The lights were still on, but she didn't care. *All the better to see you with, my dear.* Music serenaded them, but she barely heard it. Her focus was on the beautiful man she'd convinced to make love to her all night.

Before leaving Arizona, Lina had been fairly innocent about what happened sexually between men and women. She hadn't expected to sleep with or ever have sex with Mislav, although he and her parents had probably lied about that aspect of the marriage agreement, too. She'd never know. Wouldn't she have been surprised if Mislav had made it to the States and wanted her to be a true wife, including sex in the bedroom she never intended to share?

Even with only three months under her belt in Las Vegas, she'd garnered quite an education regarding sex, starting with her many roommates. None of them ever seemed to lack for male companionship when they looked up from their phones long enough to engage physically.

Lina's first roommate, Roberta, had brought a number of "boyfriends" into their closely shared room. Disregarding her presence as unimportant, Roberta and her men had proceeded to give Lina quite an education on sexual practices and the many varied positions contained therein.

She'd spent most nights facing the wall, listening with prurient curiosity, but never had enough courage to turn and watch. When Lina grumbled that she needed to sleep, Roberta suggested earplugs.

Roberta had been completely unapologetic about her vast and varied sex life with pretty much a different guy each week, explaining the endless encompassing pleasure of orgasm and how to get satisfaction for herself.

Lina hadn't known sex was supposed to be pleasurable for women until Roberta had explained the perfect sexual experience rather graphically from her well-versed perspective. Lina had never heard such explicit information in her life. But after listening to Roberta for several weeks with her variety of boyfriends, Lina longed to discover for herself lust, sex, orgasms and how it all felt.

According to all the females in her family, sexual activity was to be endured and the ultimate sacrifice women made for the joy of having children. Lina did question that, as her mother had never seemed to take much joy in her own daughter.

Naked in Dalton's strong grasp, Lina wanted to experience pleasure as her roommate had explained was due her in any sexual encounter. Dalton seemed to know what he was doing in that department. He kissed her, touched her, stroked her and generally made her feel needy and faint with every move he made.

Lina didn't know much in the way of reciprocation, but she loved everything he did for her. Side by side beneath the sheets, Lina wanted to initiate a particular position for their first sexual experience together, and hoped he'd allow it.

Roberta had recommended being on top for her very first time so she could be more in control of the movement. Lina had expressed dismay about requesting anything, thinking that her situation didn't lend itself to her having any say in what happened and she'd be too afraid to ask.

Her roommate insisted that all men simply wanted to have sex and didn't care what position they were in as long as they got off.

Lina rolled on top of Dalton, testing Roberta's resolute point about ensuring an on-top sexual position for her first time. She pulled her knees alongside Dalton's hips, breaking their exuberant kiss and staring down into his gorgeous, sultry-eyed expression.

She moved, rubbing herself intimately across the length of his erection, making his eyes close and a long groan seep from between his lips. "You are driving me absolutely crazy," he whispered.

"Am I?" She laughed. "Good." She ground herself down on him again, wanting to join with him in this position, but afraid to ask. She lowered herself to kiss his mouth, hoping to surreptitiously insert him inside her body and then ride him like she wanted.

"Wait," he said, stopping the kiss. His hands went to her hips, moving her up and away as she was about to mount him and ride like the wind.

"I was hoping we could—" she stopped talking as she heard the sound of disappointment in her own tone.

Dalton twisted, and reached toward the nightstand where his phone was. Her heart sank. When she stopped talking, he looked at her face. "You were hoping we could what?"

He grabbed his wallet, not his phone, as she tried to get out the words she wanted to say. "I was hoping I could be on top for our first time." Her heart pounded so vigorously in her chest she could hardly breathe.

Dalton pulled something small and square from his wallet. "Fine with me." He leaned up and kissed her lightly on the lips, adding off-handedly, "That's actually one of my very favorite positions."

"It is?"

"Yes. Absolutely." He held up a condom for her view. "We still need protection, regardless of position. Okay?"

Lina smiled. She'd forgotten. Her roommate's stringent rules included no sex without protection, *ever*. And that the guy brings the condom, *always*.

"Right. Protection. And you're sure you don't mind if...if I'm on top?"

She watched as he rolled the condom into place, tossing the wrapper back on the nightstand. "Of course I don't mind. I love it." He stroked his fingertips along the lengths of her thighs. "Gives me great access to things I like to touch."

His fingertips trailed up her torso, leaving electric sensations in their wake until his palm slid over and covered her breast. He squeezed her gently as the tip of her nipple poked him. She leaned down to kiss him softly, but he wrapped his arm around her and held her tight, instigating a ravenous kiss instead.

She maneuvered her hips, sliding her slick opening across his thick cock until she thought she might faint from the excitement pumping crazy and wild through her body.

Dalton let her set the pace, never once insisting on flipping her on her back to take his pleasure, as she'd seen in several movies. The type of movies she'd never been allowed to watch back home had also rounded out her education in Las Vegas on what happened between men and women.

Otherwise, Dalton practically read her mind, knowing what she wanted before she had the courage to say anything. He touched her breasts, gently squeezing her nipples as pulses of arousal zipped through her body. He stroked her back, her legs and really everywhere with expert attention. His mouth trailed along her jaw, her neck and her face repeatedly. He drove his fingers into her hair, scratching her scalp as he kissed her senseless.

She was breathless from his attention and they had only barely started. Once connected, Dalton let her move as she wished, never once trying to take charge of her demure, slow-moving pace to hurry things along.

Her confidence grew with each passing moment. She was in charge of this sexual experience and Dalton seemed delighted by her movements. Lina straightened, stared lovingly down into his face and moved her hips. She slid back and forth across his very impressive erection with a bit more gusto. It felt like he grew even bigger.

A thrill rode up and then down her spine that she was about to be as intimately connected to a man as was possible. Lina bent forward slightly to ensure the tip of his cock entered her slick body. Dalton's eyes lowered to slits as she slowly impaled herself onto his thick shaft, taking him inside slowly, inch by wickedly sensitive inch.

He filled her completely and the feeling was exactly as promised, a bit of pain but not much and a very full feeling. It was like nothing she'd ever experienced and she hadn't even started moving yet.

Lina lifted her hips and pushed back down. Dalton groaned as she moved. "You feel so..." Another groan filled in whatever he'd been about to say. His eyes closed briefly, but opened to drive a hard, sexy gaze her way. She returned the powerful look, fairly vibrating with desire as they stared at each other.

He was fully embedded. Every inch of his cock was buried to the hilt in her body. The feeling of this union was indescribably amazing even after only a few thrusts and a pause. She loved sex. She loved sex with Dalton.

Lina lifted her hips up halfway before impaling herself on him again, letting him fill her completely. She moved on him again and again, finding a steady rhythm that brought a most pleasurable sensation within.

Her movements soon sped up as she got used to his massive seductive intrusion. She searched for some indefinable way to amplify the growing ecstasy she already experienced. Moving faster up and down on him helped the euphoric, lightheaded feeling, but didn't quite bring her over the edge. She fairly pulsed with arousing desire, but didn't quite know how to peak.

When she glanced at Dalton, she saw that he watched her with an intensity that was difficult to ignore. Before she'd categorized his attitude, he moved his hand to where they were joined, his thumb touching a particularly sensitive spot, stroking her intimately. Each time he touched her there or rubbed her nub, a brazen streak of pleasure rode upward through her body, blossoming with powerful energy. She wanted more of it.

"Don't stop," she said on a moan. He grinned but didn't respond. Each gentle stroke of his thumb below accelerated some indefinable hunger.

She'd barely gotten used to his hand touching her so intimately when he squeezed her breast and his thumbnail scraped across her sensitive nipple. That small gesture ignited and released a fireball of energetic pleasure, radiating from where they were joined and racing outward to every cell in her body. A small scream escaped without warning as endless pulses spread through her.

Seconds later, Lina understood why her roommate Roberta was so vocally expressive during sex. Frenzied longing exploded within her body, bringing a newfound feeling Lina knew she'd want to experience again and again.

The next scream of delight burst from her lips before she could stop it. Her movements doubled. She moved faster and faster as wave after wave of supreme gratification rolled through her body. She could barely breathe and feel at the same time. She wanted to shriek again and again. So she did.

Lina arched backward as Dalton sped his thrusts from below, bringing her a swell of even more satisfaction with each hard stroke. After he drove his cock upward half a dozen more times, Dalton stiffened beneath her and made a noise like a satisfied growl. Together they were held as if in the very thrall of passionate gratification.

Dalton soon relaxed against the sheets. Lina slumped on top of him, unable to move, or speak, or stop breathing as fast as if she'd run a mile in record time. Regardless of her weakened state, Lina couldn't wait to do this again.

Sex was awesome. It was probably an indulgence to request a second round before coming off the high of her very first time, but that was what she intended to do. As soon as she could speak again.

CHAPTER 9

Dalton was gob smacked by Lina before, during and after this spontaneous lovemaking session. Likely he shouldn't have done it, but found it difficult to regret the best fucking sex he'd ever had in his life.

He'd certainly never been a monk where willing women were concerned. Given his excessive work schedule of late, he'd gone months without satisfactory release, making his vacation even more desired.

First on his list after *get to Las Vegas* had been *find a woman*. In the afterglow of sexual perfection, Dalton was grateful his evening had led to Lina. He certainly hadn't expected to have sex when he'd started this preliminary endeavor to find her for her family.

Lina initially seemed unschooled in the ways of love as they kissed beneath the sheets, which was a surprise, since she'd been married. She was tentative. She didn't explore. Perhaps her husband had been more traditional in his sexual prowess.

Dalton was about to ask what position she preferred when she climbed on top of him, requesting to ride him. He put one of only two condoms he currently possessed in place, hoping just the two would be enough tonight, knowing they wouldn't.

Once positioned on top, Lina was both eager and yet clearly still uncertain as they progressed, driving him crazy, sliding her slick opening across his dick before carefully impaling herself on his very happy cock. And, wow, was she tight with a capital T.

Dalton expected her to touch herself as she moved on him, but after several minutes of incredibly arousing and friction-filled thrusts, her expression seemed pensive, as if she wasn't certain what happened next. Watching her bite into her bottom lip a couple of times nearly put him over the edge.

He put his hand between them and stroked her clit a couple of times, figuring if she didn't want him to, she'd stop him. She hadn't stopped him at all. She'd moaned and whispered, "Don't stop." So he hadn't.

The overwhelming gratitude in her expression sent his heart skittering into his soul with satisfaction. Lina was getting under his skin in the best possible way. She had been since he'd seen her picture and thought she looked familiar.

Seconds after he started rubbing her clit—and with a single flick of his thumbnail across her nipple—her orgasm erupted and her silky insides squeezed his cock with repeated intensity. The expression on her face was one he'd never forget for the rest of his life. He already wanted a repeat performance well before this seductive event came to its obvious conclusion.

The shrieks of pleasure bouncing off the walls of the room told him she'd released, giving him license to do the same. The climax that rocked him hard, taking his breath away, was, in a word, extraordinary.

In the aftermath of perfection, he held her loosely when she slumped over him, wanting to stay here with her cocooned in this bed until the end of time.

Still connected intimately, Dalton rolled them until she was beneath him. Her eyes widened at first, but as they stared at each other, both of them still breathing hard, she relaxed, opening her legs wider as if to entice him.

He was incredibly tempted, but needed to clean up. He leaned forward, kissed her hard on the mouth, pulled away quickly and said, "I'll be right back." She nodded, but seemed surprised.

Dalton did what he had to and hurried back to bed. He worried she might rethink her plans, find she'd had enough and leave if he gave her too much time alone. He approached the bed and realized she hadn't moved a single bit.

She was still on her back, naked as the day she came into the world, one knee bent, the other straight, making Dalton want to return to the exact position he'd been in before. Her focus had been on the ceiling until he entered the room. Her gaze shifted to watch him move toward her.

He only had one condom left, so he climbed into bed, hugging up next to her with the intent of being charming. She was something special. He wanted to ensure she knew that.

"What are you thinking?" he asked.

The color on her cheeks suddenly deepened from rose to dark rose. "I was thinking about what just happened between us," she said quietly. Dalton put his forefinger on her soft shoulder and drew it softly and slowly down her arm. Goose bumps rose in its wake.

"Hard not to think about that." He didn't intend to sound anything but grateful and delighted, but his voice had come out low and dark.

She drilled a quick look his way. Her eyes were pensive and suddenly glassy. "Was it okay?"

"Okay?" he said, mindlessly repeating her last word.

"Did you find pleasure…with me?"

"Of course I found pleasure with you. It was the best."

"The best?" She seemed uncertain. "With me? Are you certain?"

"Yes." Dalton rolled on top of her, settled his body completely over her to get her full attention. "Of course I'm sure. Why would you doubt it?"

A sudden crushing feeling hit him square in the chest. Had she not climaxed? Fuck. He'd been so sure. "Wait. Did I not satisfy you? I'm so sorry. I thought you came." One hand slid from her waist to between her legs with the intention of immediately rectifying any deficiency on his part.

Her eyes widened again. Her soft hands fastened on his arms. "You *did* satisfy me. And... I did...have so much pleasure. It was amazing." Her palms came up, stroking both sides of his face. "Believe me. I've never felt that way before. Never."

Dalton was momentarily relieved, but felt like something was still amiss between them. "Something isn't right, though. Tell me what's on your mind. I promise not to make fun."

Lina relaxed a bit. "This experience was...my first time."

"What?" Not wanting to sound so harsh, he added, "I mean, how?" He shook his head. "You said you were married, right?"

"But I told you, he died."

"Oh...so before..." Dalton didn't want to finish his sentence. He'd taken her virginity, never once considering she hadn't had sex on her wedding night.

"My understanding was that my first husband and I were never supposed to..." She apparently didn't want to finish her sentence either. "But maybe my parents lied about that condition like they lied about many other things in the new contract, right before I ran away."

Eyes narrowing, Dalton asked, "Why did you run

from your family? You don't have to tell me, but I'm curious."

Lina shrugged. "I don't mind. The groom's parents were unhappy with the short duration of our marriage, and the lack of a family member becoming a citizen of this country as they'd planned. They wanted to substitute their younger son as a replacement, after a year of mourning. They all assumed, incorrectly, that I'd be amenable to this new plan. Well, I wasn't."

Dalton was stunned. "The second marriage was supposed to be to the brother of your recently dead husband? That's sort of cold."

She nodded, looking miserable. "Well, yes, although when you say it out loud, it sounds so much worse."

"I'm sorry, Lina."

"Don't be. That's not even the worst part. I might have been lured into their schemes for another round, but overheard my parents discussing the new conditions. They were going to tell me a whopper of a lie to get me to agree to the terms. Luckily, I found out before it was too late."

"I'm afraid to ask what you discovered."

Lina sighed. "The groom's family wanted more than citizenship for their second son. They also wanted a baby boy born within the marriage to secure the deal.

"Of course, a baby—or however many children it would take to produce a son—would tie me to the marriage, making it more difficult for me to separate and live my life the way I want. It wasn't what I'd been promised in the first contract—a two-year marriage to a man I'd have little contact with and then I could do as I pleased."

"Wow. No wonder you ran. I probably wouldn't have gone through it the first time, but my situation is different."

"Yes. I find that men often have many more choices than women."

"That's not always true, but probably more so than I've experienced. Is that why your parents want you brought back home?"

"Yes. Likely they want to bend me to their will, but I don't want to. I prefer living on my own and earning my own way. If someone makes me go back, I'll simply run again at the first opportunity."

"What makes your parents think they can persuade you?"

"Money. They have a very lucrative business. However, they value it much more than I do."

"How do they make money after the marriage?"

"Once my new husband became a citizen, he and his family would have options to make even more money, adding to their already substantial wealth in this country as well as their own. Meanwhile, my parents would forever be the ones who helped them achieve that. The marriage would bind our two families together even after a separation."

"Except that it's illegal. You'd be in trouble, too, if the authorities ever found out."

"*Alleged* trouble, if you ask my parents, and they have lawyers to help with all the details. The worst part for me in the whole sordid affair was learning what my parents were willing to do in order to get my cooperation for a second round. As if I'd bend to their will simply because they demanded it. Well, I won't."

"I'm sorry."

"I don't want to talk about this anymore."

Dalton kissed her gently. "What would you like to talk about?"

Lina stared up into his eyes with a sultry, sexy gaze that was starting to have an impact below the belt, so to speak. He settled his hips between her open thighs, careful not to go too far without protection. He leaned down and kissed her passionately. She responded with more surety this time. She was learning what he liked.

Her fingertips moved over his back, exploring his body more this time. When her hand slid perilously close to one butt cheek, he upped his game, kissing her like he wanted to devour her in one bite. She moaned into his mouth and her thighs squeezed his hips harder. Seriously, she rocked his world in every possible way.

When he drew away, the seductive gaze intensified. "You look at me like you want more. Like maybe you'll take a bite out of me if I don't satisfy you again."

"I do?" She smiled deviously. "That could very well be true. Maybe you *should* satisfy me one more time, just in case."

"I'm delighted to do that, of course, but in case of what?"

"In case we don't get the opportunity again."

He wondered if she worried about his obligation to her parents starting tomorrow morning when the banks opened at nine.

Dalton also wondered about that issue. He hadn't decided what to do as to those details.

If he went to the bank and refused the transfer of funds, would his professional obligation end? Would he have to accept payment first and then promptly transfer it back? Either way, a phone call would be necessary to explain his refusal of funds to the Dragovic family.

He could get Lina to hide out somewhere and meet him later, enabling him to tell the lie that he didn't know where she was, nor did he want to look for her, and end the arrangement with her parents. Would Ivan Dragovic take no for an answer? And even if he did, would Dalton be able to keep her safe from the phony theft charges that she didn't even know about yet?

In the morning, he'd have a long talk with Lina and explain the additional problems her father had instigated with the bogus charges. Then he'd have to hide her. The trailer in Lake Havasu came to mind as the perfect place to tuck her away and keep her out of sight. He'd also have to protect her from anyone else her family hired to find her once he turned down their offer, making him complicit in her possibly unlawful freedom.

A bounty hunter on the run from a warrant with a damsel in distress was already an alien feeling even if the summons was bogus. And he suspected it was a fake. That was the true reason he even contemplated this crazy plan.

The reversal to his normal way of thinking regarding hunting down bond jumpers might come in handy, though. Once he got her safely away, he'd press her for details on her father's ultimate intentions. He'd ensure she understood he was in this with her for the duration.

If he was going off the rails with regard to this exceptional woman, he planned to go all the way.

Lina watched several expressions cross Dalton's face before asking, "What's wrong?"

"Nothing. You're right. I'd love to take any opportunity we can." He grinned, leaning down to kiss her to quick distraction.

His hips were wedged solidly between her thighs. His cock, resting hard and heavy at her slick opening, grew steadily thicker, but he wasn't aggressive. If anything, he was exceedingly the opposite. He didn't seem in a hurry to take her again. His strength and power combined with the gentleness of his actions loosened Lina's fears to a degree.

"What do you think about this position for our second time?" she asked. "We wouldn't even have to move, at least not very much."

She pressed her hips upward, hopefully tempting him beyond all reason for a few seconds. All he had to do was shift slightly and the tip of his sizable cock would breach her slick entrance. A hollow need registered. She could get used to this and that was a dangerous desire to have. In the moment she didn't care about danger or what she *should* do. She wanted him again.

"Whatever you want, Lina." Dalton buried his face at her throat, kissing the space beneath her ear, making her crazy with need. She especially liked the sound of her name on his lips and the way he treated her with gentle respect, like he was in awe of her.

"I want you," she whispered. *Forever* was the word she didn't add to that already inflammatory statement.

Lina had never felt so secure or safe in her life. Dalton wouldn't let anything happen to her. He'd never talk her into anything she didn't want to do, at least not until he was compelled by his duty to her parents first thing in the morning, when the likely sizable funds would land in his account. Maybe he'd help her. Maybe he'd try to sway her to go back home and straighten things out. But she hoped not.

For the time being, Lina planned to enjoy herself. "I want you to make love to me as if we'll never see each other ever again, so make it good." She wrapped her arms around his neck, pulling him down for another decadent kiss.

His expression stilled. "Is that what you think? That we won't see each other ever again? I hope that isn't true."

Lina forced a smile. "Maybe I'm just not taking any chances."

Concern briefly shaped his brow. "I don't want you to worry, Lina. I'll figure something out. I promise."

She smiled, unsure what his plan included, but appreciating his willingness to help. "I'm not worried about that." She didn't know if any plan of his would work. Her father—and her mother, for that matter—could be ruthless in their efforts to make more money. Even at the expense of their only daughter.

If they had shelled out the funds to hire him, they likely wouldn't take no for an answer, regardless of what Dalton wanted to do. She smiled again, thinking that right now it seemed like he wanted to "do" her.

Lina reveled in these last few hours with Dalton. A man she could easily fall head over heels for made love to her like he expected them to be together forever, and she liked it. She wanted this feeling to last as long as possible before she enacted the escape plan she'd been pondering in the back of her mind all evening.

Dalton nibbled the space beneath her jaw, tugging her thoughts away from any plots and strategies about leaving, leading her instead to seductive pleasures and overwhelming sexual delights.

Their first time, she'd been in charge and she'd gone to town with speed and aggression to complete their ultimate experience, unsure what to expect, since it had been her first time, and then being stunned by the passionate outcome.

In this second round, Dalton was the opposite of fast. He took his time, slowly and carefully. He touched her everywhere, kissed her everywhere, licked her…everywhere until she was practically begging him to take her.

Dalton finally put another condom in place and continued to slowly make love to her, building her already volatile arousal even higher until she climaxed like a she-beast and screamed the walls down. He carefully thrust deeply and repeatedly, but with measured care, bringing her even more satisfaction than their first time together.

After she released, Dalton's expression shifted to one

of extreme male pride, right before he sped his hip thrusts strikingly, and soon stiffened, his face tightening in pleasure or pain or perhaps both. His eyes dipped shut and he groaned deeply as pulse after pulse of pleasure radiated outward from their intimate union. He stopped moving his hips and settled his lower half heavy between her open thighs.

Lina floated on a cloud of complete gratification. The sweet scent of their lovemaking filled the air around them with every breath she took, enflaming her yet again. She was completely covered by a man she was falling in love with, wondering at the crazy notion of love at first sight. Perhaps that wasn't the fable she'd always believed it was.

Dalton remained balanced on his elbows, breathing hard, his wide eyes staring at her with an intensity she found mesmerizing. He looked like he wanted to capture her soul. She wanted to let him, if only she wasn't about to go back on the run. She closed her eyes, breaking the gaze, wishing things could be different so she could remain with this amazing, sexy man.

They showered together in his luxurious bath. Lina was awash in sensations. He brought her to a vibrant third pleasurable peak with his tongue after scrubbing her clean with a soft washcloth.

He then soaped her once more, rinsed her carefully, dried her off and carried her to bed. She'd been boneless after her third orgasm. Dalton followed her beneath the sheets, snuggling in with her, wrapping his arms around her and kissing the back of her neck. It would be so easy to just fall into his protective arms and let him take care of her.

Lina was so relaxed she barely remained conscious, probably dozing a couple times for a minute or two, but the clock on the nightstand filled her view when her eyes opened and also amplified her focus. Their time together—cuddled close, naked and satisfied in a post-lovemaking stupor—ticked down. Trepidation grew in her heart with each passing moment. The fear of going back to a life with her parents and their endless expectations woke her fully.

She considered the plan she'd concocted piecemeal in between one orgasm and another. A stealthy strategy, where no one would ever think to look for her in the place she planned to go. Not even Dalton, she hoped.

Lina trusted Dalton to a degree, but not enough to stay with him if he had to answer to her parents in the morning. He might want to protect her, but he didn't understand the lengths to which her father would go to ensure his wishes were carried out. She didn't want to count on Dalton only to discover he'd underestimated her family's greed.

They'd already spent quite a bit of money on expensive investigation agencies to track her down. No one had found her until Dalton.

If he helped her, or even mentioned finding her and letting her go, it would put him in her father's dangerous sights. And if he didn't let her go or, worse, turned her over to her parents because of his initial contract, that would break her heart.

Her only choice was to sneak away before the bank opened.

Lina pretended to sleep, waiting for Dalton to nod off. It didn't take long. She counted to five hundred, letting him get deeply asleep before attempting to shift out of his strong arms.

Lina carefully moved away from Dalton's warm body and out of the bed. That small feat accomplished, she dressed in the dark, grabbed her belongings and eased out of the room. This was absolutely the most difficult part of her plan—leaving Dalton behind without daring to utter a single word of farewell or attempting to steal one final kiss, although she wanted the latter more than anything.

In the hallway, she walked quietly to the stairs and hustled down three flights before getting on the elevator and heading for the lobby. Once the elevator doors opened to the lobby, she turned and exited out the back of the hotel and away from the main strip, securing a taxi at the lonely cab stand there.

Directing the driver to the address of the nearest library—she knew them all by heart—Lina walked to an all-night restaurant, seeking coffee and a healthy boost to keep going. With a lidded to-go cup filled to the brim, she walked five blocks to the bus station, and purchased a ticket. She only had a couple of hours to wait until the bus departed.

For the moment, luck was on her side. She sipped her coffee, missing Dalton, hating to have left the way she did. It couldn't be helped.

She took the departure time as a sign that she was on the right track, even as her heart throbbed in pain at leaving Dalton behind, warm and cozy and in bed.

It took the bulk of her meager funds tucked away in the fake bathroom cleaner can, but she needed to disappear. She might be able to trust Dalton, but her father was another matter.

If it was even hinted that Dalton had seen her in Las Vegas, a swarm of people who owed her father favors big and small would descend on the city to search behind every cactus and in each desert crevasse with the instructions to drag her back home.

She'd be hauled back to Arizona and married off to Marko Zupan as soon as possible. She doubted the Zupans would want to wait the full year of mourning if it meant Lina might run again. And she would, any chance she got.

The truth was, she'd run even if they succeeded in

marrying her off to Mislav's younger brother. She'd have to. She would never leave any child of hers behind while she fled whatever her circumstances ended up being.

She knew it. They knew it.

Therefore, her *only* option was to run, stay out of reach and keep from being taken back home at all costs.

Chapter 10

Dalton woke after a night filled with sublime pleasure to the sound of his phone vibrating on the nightstand. He squinted, opening only one eye to check the time, before lifting his phone to his ear. It was early. Not even light yet.

"What," he said as civilly as possible.

"Where are you?" The terse tone of his handler, Miles Turner, came through the line like an unwanted telemarketer interrupting dinner.

"On vacation," Dalton muttered, closing his eyes and sinking back into the comfortable sheets, burrowing one side of his face into his pillow. "I know you got the memo. You signed it."

"Didn't the Dragovic family contact you about a private job?" Miles asked, sounding surprised.

"How do you know about that?" Dalton didn't open his eyes, but perked up ever so slightly at the unexpected reference to the Dragovics. Actually wondering how Miles *knew* about things was a big waste of time in the long run.

"I may have sent them in your direction when pressured by some folks wanting to call in favors," Miles admitted.

"Awesome. Thanks." Dalton relaxed again. Now he knew how the Dragovics had found him at least. They were going to end up disappointed. Dalton wouldn't take Lina to her parents if she didn't want to go.

Memories of the night before filtered into his sleepy, well-satisfied brain. Lina on top of him. Lina beneath him. Lina in the shower with him. Lina snuggled up with him. Every visual was more enticing than the one before, making him wish he had another condom. Maybe he'd take a quick trip down to the lobby and purchase a big box of protection and tuck in for the week. He'd also have to blow off her family and their offer, but right now that sounded like a great and restful vacation idea.

Once he was fully conscious, he needed to stop thinking about sex and start thinking about someplace safe to stash her so no one else could find her.

The charges her family had filed against her might be problematic, but he planned to read the language of the warrant carefully. Perhaps there was a loophole he could take advantage of to keep Lina safe for longer than hiding out would accomplish.

"Do you think you can locate her?" Miles asked in his ear. He'd almost dozed off again.

"Who?"

"Nikolina Dragovic." Miles sounded exasperated.

Dalton's eyes opened again. "What do you know about her?"

"I know her parents are desperately searching for her. They have been for a few months. However, recently they also swore out a warrant for her to be located and brought back to testify as to her knowledge of some stolen family goods."

That was not the way the warrant had been explained to him, as if it masqueraded as a subpoena. "Did you read it? The warrant, I mean."

"Maybe. Why?"

"Any way to get out of it?"

"Out of the warrant?"

Dalton ignored the sound of disbelief in Miles's tone. "Yes. Like a technicality that wouldn't allow her to be brought in for some reason." There was silence on the line for so long Dalton thought Miles had hung up.

"What the fuck are you doing, Dalton?"

"Nothing. Not yet, anyway." He reached out to the other side of the bed without looking, searching for Lina. When they'd fallen asleep, she'd been snuggled up close. He didn't feel her now. Where was she? He glanced over one shoulder and saw that he was alone in bed. Her side of the bed was empty.

Hmm. Bathroom, maybe? He ran a hand down his face on the off chance it would help him wake up faster.

He hadn't felt her leave, although two rounds of exceptional sex had transpired, making him more relaxed than he'd been in months. It was a wonder he was any part of coherent now. He put his hand down on the sheets again, expecting to feel residual warmth from her recent departure. The fabric was cold, no longer warm from her body heat.

Dalton sat up, looking at Lina's side of the bed as if for the first time. Realizing it was truly empty. *That* woke him up. He scanned the room, listening for her, hearing nothing. Not a sound. Was she gone? How long had she been gone? Where? Ice? He glanced at the clock. At this hour? No. Was she okay?

He leapt from the bed, searching the entire room more thoroughly, racing into the bathroom, tearing back the shower curtain.

Nothing. Empty. Gone.

He marched to the closet where he'd put her things the night before. The slider was ajar. He knew he'd left it completely closed. A panicked feeling rose quickly as he opened it, knowing what he'd find.

Nothing. Empty. Gone.

Miles had been talking in his ear the whole time he fruitlessly searched the room, but Dalton hadn't heard a single word. Well, the gist had been about his career and the diplomatic notion of doing things he didn't want to for the sake of making nice and gathering favors. Blah. Blah. Blah. None of which he was interested in right now.

"Are you even listening to me?" Miles asked. The exasperation was now unmistakable in his voice.

"No." He needed to get dressed and search for Lina before he couldn't track her. She was in danger and didn't even know it. He mentally cursed himself for not telling her everything her father had said last night before lust and sex and more sex had fried his brain.

"Okay. I get it," Miles said. "I ruined your vacation. But you should seriously consider taking the Dragovic job. They could be a powerful ally for you one day if you can find their daughter."

I already found her. Then I did wicked things to her. And then I lost her. "No."

"Don't be so difficult."

"No."

Miles started talking again, but Dalton ignored him. He searched briefly for a note, but knew he wouldn't find one. She was smart and strong, but he hadn't told her about the warrant.

Lina was out there, and more vulnerable than she realized because he'd been too busy having sex with her to tell her of the danger he'd discovered during the conversation with her father. "I've got to go."

"Dalton. Wait. There is something else."

"What?"

"If you won't do the Dragovics a favor, do one for me. I have a job in Arizona tomorrow that begins as a journey and will ultimately end in Las Vegas with a scheduled meeting. Once you're done, you can go back to your vacation."

"No. Absolutely not."

"What if it's an emergency?"

"Then you do it. You're already in Arizona. Tell you what—if you come to Las Vegas tomorrow we can hang out or have a drink together before I leave on my next vacation adventure. But just keep in mind that I may not be here long or even until tomorrow." *I'm out the door in twenty seconds.*

"Where are you going next?"

Dalton laughed. "I'm not telling you that, Miles." He retrieved his clothing and prepared to end the call.

"Dalton—" Miles said in a particular tone he used to be persuasive.

"No. Don't *Dalton* me. You can't guilt me into this. I'm on vacation. I'm not coming off to do anything for anyone. No journeys. No building favors for my career. No finding anyone, even for Ivan Dragovic. When he calls later, I'm begging off the case. And if you call again, I won't pick up."

"Don't be a dick."

"Back at ya."

"Fine. I'll do this Arizona-to-Las Vegas job myself. But fair warning—it might be a good idea not to blow off Ivan Dragovic."

"Whatever."

"He's powerful and he usually gets his way. If you don't take the job, fine, I guess, but let him down gently. Do you even know the meaning of the word diplomatic? If not, you need to find a dictionary and look it up."

"Very funny."

"I'm not laughing. He's someone you *never* want as an enemy."

"Noted." Dalton pondered the idea of Ivan Dragovic ever finding out he'd been Lina's first lover. Was that an offense punishable by death in the Dragovic household? Even if it cost him his life, it had been worth it. He'd thoroughly enjoyed the experience and hoped to do it again. Maybe he had a death wish. Or maybe he was falling hard for a certain smart, sexy runaway.

Dalton put his clothes on, grabbed his wallet, phone and keys and headed for the door. Then he stopped. He shouldn't rush off without a plan. He forced himself to take a deep breath and let it out slowly.

He took the precious time to walk outside onto the terrace to collect his thoughts. Dalton seated himself in the chair Lina had occupied the night before and thought about what she would do. He did his best to get inside her head and figure out where she might go.

Where would she think of as safe? Dalton considered everything he knew about her. He conjured up every conversation they'd had in their short acquaintance, and put himself in her shoes.

She'd been hidden away under a pseudonym, working and living quietly in a city known for being flashy and loud. Now she was on the run again. She had to know he'd look for her. And she knew her father was hunting for her as well, but because Dalton had been distracted by sex last night, she didn't understand the lengths her father had already gone to locate her.

Damn it, he should have mentioned the warrant, but knew in his soul that if he had she might have bolted well before longing, lust and lovemaking had ensued.

Not a good enough reason in retrospect, but Dalton had a hard time regretting their amazingly passionate time together. Sultry, sexy visions and seductive sounds from the night before intruded on his calm. He was ruined.

Dalton glanced at the sky. It was still dark. The sun wouldn't be fully over the distant mountains, creating the sunrise for several more hours. She had her things from her apartment, so she was ready to go. Lina could be headed absolutely anywhere.

Wait, that wasn't true. She had mentioned her limited finances. She hadn't wanted to pay for a motel. He remembered the first time he'd seen her. The picture with her long dark hair in a ponytail surfaced like a phantom in the night, teasing him and making him smile. He remembered where she'd been in that photo.

And he *knew* exactly where she was. By the time he got to his car, he had also figured out where she might go to hide and used his phone to check the departing bus schedule for both area transit companies. He grinned like a loon when he saw a bus headed for the destination he sought leaving Las Vegas in just over an hour. The station was only a few miles away.

Dalton encountered little traffic on his drive to the bus station, making better time than he expected. Before going inside, he snagged a parking spot close to the entrance. He walked into the small station and spotted her right away in the quiet waiting area.

Lina faced away from the door, but he'd know her anywhere. He'd be able to spot the color of her hair alone from twenty paces. She turned and he saw her brief profile as she sipped from a disposable coffee cup, blissfully unaware he'd found her.

The bus leaving for Lake Havasu was listed as an on-time departure in less than an hour. They'd start loading up the bus twenty minutes or so before leaving the terminal. He only had half an hour to convince her to stick with him.

He slowed his gait, not wanting to scare her or take away her semi-relaxed posture. The moment she saw him, she'd tense and possibly run. He didn't want to chase her down. Not in public, anyway.

Dalton sat in the row directly behind her, the backs of their chairs mashed together. He turned sideways in the molded seat, staring at the back of her head for a few moments before disturbing her calm.

"You forgot to say goodbye," he said in a low tone by way of an opening.

Her head whipped around, her face registered shock, and the serene posture she'd had was gone. She sat straight up, her lovely spine going rigid.

Dalton gave her props for not bolting the second she saw him. In fact, she relaxed a bit into her seat with a resigned-sounding sigh. "How did you find me?"

He grinned. "That's what I do. I find people. Do you understand now how good I am at it?"

She squinted and looked down at her clothing. "Do you have a tracker on me or something?"

"No. But that would have been a great idea. I just didn't have the time or the equipment with me to make it happen." He smiled. She did not.

"Are you making fun of me again?"

"No, of course not. I'm actually very impressed with you."

"I don't know why. I'm not so impressive that I fooled you."

He lifted one of his shoulders in a shrug. "I'm hard to fool. Goes along with my awesome people-finding skills."

"Listen, Dalton. I'm *not* going back home. I appreciate that you helped me out last night." She paused, gazing into his eyes, and added, "but if you try to take me out of here, I'll scream. And I'll scream loud enough to bring the rafters down."

"Don't do that." He looked around at the low-volume crowd in the station. He didn't want to attract any unnecessary attention. "I promise. I won't try to take you out of here because I know exactly how loud you can scream." The memory of her orgasmic cries filled him with delight. His reference must have hit home. Her cheeks filled with color in an instant.

"Why are you here if you aren't going to take me back home?"

"I failed to tell you something important last night. Something you need to know regardless of whether we stay together, but I'm hoping you'll consider all of your options."

She shook her head dismissively at first, as if nothing he had to say would be worthy of tracking her down in this high-handed manner. But when he said the word "options," she pushed out a long, heavy sigh. "Okay, tell me. What do I need to know? What options should I consider?"

He leaned closer and lowered his voice. "Your father has had a warrant put out on you in conjunction with some stolen family jewelry."

Her mouth fell open and her brows narrowed instantly. It looked like she had no idea what he was talking about. He was more certain than ever that the charges had been trumped up.

"That's a lie. I didn't steal anything from them."

"I believe you. However, it's safe to say I'm not the only one searching for you, and I'm fairly certain no one else will be convinced of that."

Lina shouldered her backpack and reached for her bags. She looked a second away from bolting out of the bus station like a cartoon roadrunner, leaving only a few puffs of smoke in her wake.

"Wait," Dalton said, putting a hand on her shoulder. "Listen, before you go wildly off on your own. I haven't seen the warrant. I don't know whether you are to be arrested as a suspect or simply brought to authorities for questioning as a witness, but either way, if any law enforcement agency or entity recognizes you, they *will* take you back to Arizona and to your family post haste."

Her cheeks had paled as he spoke. "How do you know?"

"Your father told me when he called last night. I also had another person verify the information before coming here."

Her lovely gaze narrowed. "Why didn't you tell me about the warrant last night?"

"I'm sorry. I meant to but—" Dalton stopped and gazed deeply into her eyes.

"But what?"

"But...well, we were busy, twice. And I fell asleep."

The blush came up in her cheeks again and threatened to make him soft in the head. She was so beautiful. He was captivated by her spirit and her strong motivation and her smarts and he shouldn't be, unless he intended to ignore her father and pursue her. His desire to make a place for her in his life was way ahead in points of completing the job to bring her home.

"I'm sorry I didn't inform you of the warrant. But I intended to tell you later today, possibly over breakfast. Also, I thought we were going to work together." He tried not to reveal how disappointed he'd been to find her gone after their blissful evening.

Lina looked away. "I didn't know you'd decided to side with me over my father. Many wouldn't make a choice like that. No one I've heard of ever has, in fact. I didn't want to take the chance. I was afraid you'd choose the less dangerous path and take me back to my parents."

"You still thought that, even after what happened between us last night? I obviously did not do a good enough job of expressing my feelings."

"I..." She stopped talking and pushed out a long sigh. "I have quite a lot to lose if I trust the wrong person."

"Lina, you *can* trust me," Dalton said quietly.

Sadness seemed to cast a shadow over her. Her shoulders sagged. "I can't even trust my parents or anyone else in my family. Why should I trust you?" Her eyes watered up and a tear slipped from the corner of one eye. She sniffed and turned away from him.

"For starters, last night wasn't some meaningless hookup for me. I care about you. Did you believe our time together was only a one-night stand?"

She opened her mouth, shut it and shook her head. "It doesn't matter what I believe."

"It matters to me." Dalton hadn't ever felt like this with any other woman. The sex alone had been stupendous and everything he'd ever dreamed of having in a future mate. They hadn't discussed it, because she hadn't made a big deal out of it, but being her first lover also *meant* something to him.

Dalton wasn't someone who believed in love at first sight, but this was as close as he'd ever come to believing in the notion. He liked her. He was impressed by her strength and her motivation to live on her own terms. She was resilient and beautiful and not spoiled in any way, shape or form, unlike what he'd once suspected of someone in her situation and the family she'd been brought up in.

"To answer your question, no. You weren't some meaningless onetime hookup. I care for you, too. You've been in my thoughts for a while. The truth is, I remembered you from three months ago when you chased that man out of the casino. I thought about you more than a few times, wondering if you'd ever come back. I may have even looked for you on occasion." She shrugged and her smile indicated her apprehension about admitting it.

Dalton smiled, thinking back to that moment as well. Her hair had still been long and dark. He'd watched as she approached, looked away, trying not to be obvious about finding her attractive, but couldn't help looking at her again. He turned in time to see her pull the band from her ponytail, allowing her hair to cascade around her shoulders. Extraordinary.

Dalton had marched up to speak to her, wanting to hear her voice, using the picture as an ice-breaker.

"Have you seen this guy around here anywhere, by chance?" he asked briskly, not expecting any positive answer. But her eyes had widened, and without speaking she'd pointed to the guy he'd been searching for seated in a booth right inside the restaurant, pretty as you please. The culprit had looked up exactly in that moment and had seen Dalton with Lina pointing at him. A millisecond later, he was off like a shot.

Dalton left the beautiful girl behind and chased his target through the restaurant and out into the casino. The dumbass soon raced down the Strip and he'd had to exert everything he had to catch the idiot. By the time he caught his breath, processed his bounty with the police and returned to the restaurant, she was gone and he didn't see her again until three months later, in a photo of a runaway rich girl. He didn't completely connect the dots until seated on the terrace today.

Lina smiled at him. "After I pointed out that guy, I watched you all the way until you entered the restaurant. I also watched you chase him out of the casino." She was blushing again.

Dalton reached out and grabbed her hand, caressing her palm with his thumb. She didn't pull away. She started to relax again.

He leaned closer, catching a whiff of her scent mixed with the lemon soap from the hotel shower the night before. "Miss Smith, are you trying to tell me that you stared at my ass for some length of time after we spoke to each other months ago?"

CHAPTER 11

Lina laughed out loud. The sound of her exuberant joy echoed across the waiting area of the mostly empty bus station. She nodded, his good-natured teasing sincerely making her question ever leaving him behind in that warm, cozy hotel bed.

"Yes. I stared at your butt from the time you ran into the restaurant until you chased him out of the casino. And I'd do it again."

Dalton Langston, Security Specialist, was a difficult man to ignore, especially after she'd spent such a wickedly satisfying night with him. Her opening salvo into the realm of sexual experiences would forever be cast as perfect.

"All that time you were staring?" he asked, a devilish smile dancing around his lips. "I'm flattered."

"Yes. Well, your derrière was very worthy of my attention."

"Good to know."

Lina remembered thinking about the gorgeous stranger later that night as Roberta and her flavor of the week were going at it hot and heavy, loud and exuberant only a few feet away.

Sleep had been a long time coming. Lina's first

epiphany regarding sexual attraction had given her a sleepless night. She hadn't remembered his face, beyond thinking him very handsome, but she'd never forgotten his butt.

"Three months later you did basically the same thing, only this time, I was the one in the picture."

"Did you stare at my butt this time, too?"

"I stared at all of you." If they'd been alone, she'd already be kissing him.

A speaker above them squawked, distracting her from her reverie about Dalton's fine derrière and his sultry kisses. A voice announced in a monotone that her bus would be boarding in fifteen minutes.

She looked up at the sound and then back at Dalton's handsome face. Lina couldn't believe he'd found her. She hadn't even known where she was going until after she left his hotel room. Perhaps she needed to relax and partner with someone. It would certainly be nice not to run for her life all alone.

Dalton was an exceptional hunter of people, but the way he kept finding her, and offering to help her instead of subduing her and hauling her back to her parents, made her feel special and safe and happy and a little bit loved for the first time in a long time.

Her parents defined love as doing what they thought was best for her. Maybe they did love her in their own way. She had no doubt they believed they had her best interests at heart, but their true foundation was built on financial gain and the idea that she'd one day be part of the family's shady enterprises.

She wanted no part of it, but they couldn't understand the concept of a child of theirs not wanting their wealthy lifestyle, regardless of what came along as possible criminal baggage.

The primary reason she agreed to the farce of a wedding at all was because she had hoped to pawn

Mislav off on her parents as a surrogate child in her stead. Something amusing occurred to her. Perhaps if her parents adopted Mislav's brother they could simply cut her out as the middleman. Maybe she should suggest it as a serious proposition to make everyone happy.

They wanted a member of the recently befriended Zupan family—a male, most importantly—to head up their business interests and Lina didn't want to have any part in it, ever. Win-win.

She wanted to travel the world, go places where people didn't know her before she introduced herself. She would love to shop quietly without everyone she met on a day-to-day basis knowing exactly whose daughter she was and promptly shy away for fear of retribution for any number of minor offenses, or worse, making friends with her in the hopes of getting an "in" with her family.

Unfortunately, it wasn't that simple. According to long-standing tradition, her parents wanted a marital connection to attain their prized son-in-law to run their business.

Lina squeezed Dalton's hand. "If I head for Lake Havasu, no one will think to look for me there. I can't believe you did. But most importantly, *they* won't, exactly like they never would have looked for me in Las Vegas."

Dalton's eyes narrowed. "Maybe, but I don't know about the other man who found you outside your apartment building right before you came to save my apparently praiseworthy ass." She smiled inwardly as he continued. "And if he's been hired by your parents, there may be others, and I don't know the level of skills those entities possess.

"Because something truly awesome happened to me recently, I haven't had a chance to check anything out yet. Someone distracted me last night in the best possible way." He smiled again, tugging on her hand lightly. "Please come with me, Lina. I can protect you. I *will* protect you."

She shook her head. "It has little to do with my thoughts on your ability to protect me. The truth is, I spent a lot of my money on a ticket to Lake Havasu, and I'm going there."

Dalton's gaze zeroed uncomfortably into hers. "Do you remember the name of the campground where my trailer is?"

Lina felt her cheeks heat up as she lowered her eyes. She *did* remember. His place in Lake Havasu was her ultimate destination.

She'd been planning to sweet-talk her way into his place by posing as a sister or girlfriend coming ahead to meet him. If that didn't work, she'd break in. She did have some rather felonious skills she'd never put into practice, thanks to a childhood spent with Petra's older and semi-lawless brother helping her knowledge along.

"Coyote Willow, right?" Lina said, still without looking at him.

"That's right." He must have guessed her intentions, because he added, "I'm curious as to how you planned to gain entrance to my RV."

She shrugged. "I was going to tell them I was your sister and you'd forgotten to give me a key."

Dalton laughed. "Too bad I don't have any sisters and really too bad that the owner of the campground knows that. Not to mention that the rental isn't under my real name. You would have been evicted before you got inside."

"I guess it's too late to ask you the name it's under." She looked into his gorgeous face, raising her eyebrows in question.

He smiled but didn't answer.

"Not a single sister, huh?"

"Nope. I have four older brothers, technically."

"Technically?" Lina assumed he referenced stepbrothers or half-brothers. She didn't have time to ask before his attention was drawn away by something behind her.

A ferocious frown appeared on Dalton's face. He leaned forward, gaze darting to her eyes in either anger or panic.

Oh no. Now what?

Dalton saw the door to the bus station pop open before he could explain that his twin, Deke, was older by ten minutes. Technically correct, but annoying all the same since they were the same age.

He'd been sidetracked, trying to talk her out of using her very clever bus ticket purchase, when a well-dressed man with a funny walk entered the station. He marched across the tile lobby with a determined, if odd-looking, stride, taking Dalton's focus away from Lina.

The newcomer looked very out of place in the bus station. He wore an expensive suit and with each step, he limped enough to be noticeable, like a guy with a bad prostate. The man hadn't seen them yet. Dalton had a bad feeling all of a sudden.

"Lina," Dalton whispered quickly. "Trust me and duck down in your seat, right now!" She let go of his hand and slid to the floor on the other side of the row of seats.

Dalton put his hand up to his face as if he were trying to catch some sleep before boarding his bus, watching the man between his spread fingers. The man stopped moving, parked himself near the center of the waiting room and scanned it carefully twice more before turning to limp back outside.

"What's going on?" Lina whispered from her cross-legged seat on the concrete floor.

Dalton stood up, but motioned for her to stay where she was. "Stay right there. I'm going to check on something."

The voice over the speaker announced the Lake Havasu bus would start pre-boarding in five minutes for an on-time departure in twenty-five. Dalton caught her eye again. "Don't move. I'll be right back."

Casually, Dalton crossed to a side door leading to the parking lot. Three men stood right outside the front doors, staring at the parking lot. One was the flashily dressed man with the limp, the other two sported bruises and cuts Dalton could see from thirty feet away. One he recognized from his fight last night after following Lina home from the library.

Mr. Flashy Suit pointed toward the area where Dalton's car was parked. One of the men headed in that direction. The other was directed back inside the bus station. Dalton headed there himself, making a beeline for Lina before the other man entered.

He walked quickly to where she was still seated on the floor, squatted down and said, "Here's the plan. We need to get out of here without being seen. The front door is out of the question and once outside, we'll have to walk because my car is currently under surveillance."

"Who is it?"

"Two of the guys are beat up and look very much like two thirds of the three I tangled with last night. The third guy that stepped in here to look around is walking with a limp like he got kicked in the nuts recently. Sound familiar to you?"

She sucked in a breath and tried to stand.

"Wait," he said. The guy with a vivid bruise on his face walked across the foyer and headed toward the bathrooms.

Once he was out of sight, Dalton helped her grab her luggage and they made for the side door. Dalton peeked out. Mr. Flashy Suit and the other man were walking across the parking lot toward Dalton's SUV.

"They definitely found my vehicle. How did you get here?"

"I walked from the nearest library."

"Any thoughts on how we can get away faster than on our feet?" They'd have to pass by the dangerous-looking trio to get to the taxi stand on the other side of the main entrance.

Lina paused, looked around and pointed at the street. "There." She tugged on his hand and together they headed at a fast clip away from the parking lot toward the road.

Half a block away, Dalton saw a city bus approaching the stop at the end of the sidewalk. They were practically running as the bus came to a hissing stop and popped open the doors in time for them to board.

Lina pulled cash from her bag and handed the driver exact fare for both of them, also asking for the next stop location. The driver told them the bus was bound for the opposite end of the Strip.

There were only five other people on board and they were all seated toward the rear, near the other exit. Lina moved down the aisle, taking the fourth seat on the right, by the window. He followed and started to sit beside her. She shook her head and pointed at the seats across the aisle.

"We don't want to look like we're together."

"Right." Dalton smiled. "You are one smart chick-a-roo." He seated himself in the aisle seat, leaning forward slightly to keep Lina clearly in view.

"Thanks. I think. Where should we head?"

"The Strip."

"Specifically."

"Car rental place on the north end. Why? Did you have another destination in mind?"

Given the way he knew he was staring at her, and the fact she'd paid their fares, they might as well be sitting together. Anyone with eyes would be able to see that they were together, but he played along and remained in his seat.

"Is the car rental place near the Little White Chapel, where they have twenty-four-hour drive-through weddings?" Lina asked.

Dalton's gaze narrowed. "Maybe. Why?"

Lina turned her head and grinned. Dalton thought his heart might stop just witnessing her sheer beauty. "I thought of a great idea that would make me feel completely safe with you."

Dalton softened. There wasn't much he wouldn't do to keep her...or keep her smiling.

"Would you be willing to marry me?" Her dazzling smile distracted him from the meaning of her words for a moment.

Wait. What?

CHAPTER 12

Lina watched Dalton carefully for any hint that he didn't have her best interests at heart. Her plan was audacious, she knew that. But his initial split-second reaction was reassuring, like perhaps he was a little bit awestruck at the idea of marrying her instead of repulsed.

Dalton looked nearly jubilant for half a second before the meaning of her words settled in. "Marry you?"

"Yes. We could even do the drive-through for expedient service, if you want."

His expression shifted to disbelief, hands gesturing around him. "What, in this bus? Think they'd toss out their rigid schedule for our quickie nuptials, do you?" The grin that followed warmed her heart.

"Are you making fun of me again?"

He shook his head. "Of course not. I'm just wondering if we have to hijack the bus for your plan to work. Don't get me wrong. I'm game either way."

She shrugged. "I guess we can simply walk inside and get married, as disappointing as it will be to forgo the drive-through dream wedding I'd planned."

Dalton looked out the window at the lit-up Strip outside. The skies were dark, but the neon lights kept everything bright as day here. They were well away from the bus station. He made a command decision and moved to sit next to her.

"Now people will think we're together if they see us. Is this a wise move?" She didn't shy away from him, though.

He grabbed her hand, placing it between his roughened palms. "I doubt we've been fooling anyone since climbing on this bus. If we're about to tie the knot, Vegas style, sweetheart, we *are* together and everyone will see us anyway."

"Is that what we are about to do?" She pursed her lips in mock puzzlement. "Honestly, I thought you'd put up more of a fight to keep your bachelorhood intact."

Dalton laughed. "Shows what you know. I've been on the hunt for a wife for months."

She did look surprised. "Really? Why is that?"

"I'm the only unmarried guy in my family." He glanced in her direction, a sexy half-smile lifting one corner of his luscious mouth. "I guess you'll do in a pinch."

She snatched her hand away, shifting closer to the window and turned away from him to look at nothing. It was a foolish idea. She shouldn't be unhappy that he didn't want to throw his life away on a formerly rich, well-known, alleged mobster's daughter turned invisible food runner with a fake name.

His low, sexy laugh came next as he moved closer. The scent of him made her insides melty and filled with longing. The nearer he got, the more she wanted him. He leaned in until he was able to gently kiss the side of her face. And then he did it again. Lina's eyes closed and sweet pulses of sensation burst beneath her skin wherever his lips touched her.

Dalton kissed the space next to her ear, whispering, "I'm just kidding. I'd be honored to marry you, Lina. I do want to protect you. What better way than by making you my bride?"

"How can I trust that? I think you are making fun of me again."

"No. I'm not making fun. But if we're about to get married so that I can protect you, I'd say we have to trust each other, don't you think?" He kissed her again. Soon he trailed his lips down to her jaw, her neck, and beneath her ear. The sensation was making her crazy with desire.

"Perhaps it was a foolish notion on my part."

"Why did you suggest it then?"

"My parents want to marry me off to enrich their coffers, but their plan is all about how they want me to live my life and not how I wish to live it."

"I see. And how do you want to live your life?"

"I want to travel. I want to see the world. I don't want their money or their lifestyle or to carry on their extensive and infamous family holdings. I'm willing to work for what I have, even if I never have very much."

A low rumble of laughter escaped Dalton's throat, giving her a quick thrill. "That's even more reason to fall for you, Lina. I also want to travel. While I've seen a lot of the world, nothing would give me greater pleasure than to show you all of my favorite places. Not to mention that I'm also someone who's willing to work hard to ensure my life is my own."

"Your job is a bounty hunter, yes? You find people for a living all over the world and then bring them in?"

"More or less, but I recently took a job with a security firm to curtail so much travel."

"But I thought you loved to travel."

"Oh, I do. Unfortunately, most of the people I chase don't hide out in nice places."

She grinned. "So you took a new job?"

"Yes. And while the new employment is still fairly demanding, I've taken steps recently to simplify it so I could settle down and find a kindred spirit to join me."

"I wouldn't have a problem with your traveling, if you promised to hurry home to me. Or maybe you could take me with you sometimes." She spoke as if they were about to have a real wedding, a real marriage. Was she crazy? Undoubtedly. But then so was he, because he seemed to like her ideas.

"Having someone understand my need to be on the road for work would be precious to me. Of course I'd hurry home to you or gladly bring you along, if I felt it was safe enough for you."

Lina squeezed his hand. "So does this mean you will marry me?"

"Yes. Let's get married."

Her expression was so exquisitely beautiful, Dalton wanted to take a mental photo and put it alongside the one from the bus station in Flagstaff. "One more consideration."

"What?"

"Should Elvis be the one to marry us, or not so much?"

She laughed. "Honestly, I don't care as long as I don't have to run from my parents' scheming any longer. Also, you are a good person, and I like you. You make me feel safe. Marrying someone I have chosen based on my feelings would be a monumental boon."

"And the sex is great."

"I think it is exceptional."

"So do I." He looked at her like he wished they were alone. He looked like he would do wicked things to her if they were. She grinned as the bus slowed and approached their stop.

Dalton jumped up, helped her carry her things and they got off their escape bus a block away from a twenty-four-hour car rental place.

Unfortunately, there were only three vehicles not on

reserve for customers. The flashy red sports car was too conspicuous and likely didn't have enough space for her few bags. The humongous black SUV that seated nine people comfortably was the one he seemed to want, but he shook his head at that one as well. It was too noticeable, apparently, like the sports car. That left the obscure beige four-door sedan.

"Do you at least have a sedan with six cylinders instead of four?" Dalton asked.

The pimple-faced clerk shook his head. "You're lucky we have this many choices. There's a convention in town." His voice cracked twice as he gave the bad news.

"There's always a convention in town," Dalton grumbled under his breath as he handed the clerk his credit card and signed the rental agreement for the beige sedan.

"Don't worry. This is great news," Lina whispered, wrapping her arms around his left bicep.

"Why's that? I'd love some great news for a change."

"Now that we have a rental car, we can go to the drive-through chapel and get that dream wedding I wanted so much."

A wicked smile wreathed Dalton's luscious mouth as he signed his name with a flourish, shoved the papers across the counter and turned to kiss her square on the lips. He did not have a problem with public displays of affection. She liked that about him, among many other things.

Once inside their rental vehicle, Dalton headed straight for the nearest drive-through wedding chapel.

There was a couple ahead of them just finishing up their nuptials. Dalton parked behind their ribbon-festooned vehicle and they gathered the papers and things they'd need based on a list posted on the outer wall of the chapel.

"Am I marrying Emma Smith?" Dalton asked.

"No. I want it to be a real marriage with my real name."

"Do you have identification?" He seemed surprised when she nodded. "I thought I read in a report that you left your Nikolina Dragovic identification behind at your parents' house when you left."

"I did. You will be marrying Nikolina Zupan."

His eyes widened. "Right. How did you get *that* identification so fast?"

"It was part of the proxy papers I signed once I was married. The lawyer handed me a bunch of papers once it was over. I saved them and brought them with me."

"Proxy papers from a lawyer? Where was your groom?"

"In Kzeratia. The Zupans sent a proxy agent to ensure we were married on a particular date, per the agreement."

"So are you saying that you never even met the guy you were married to so briefly?"

"Correct."

"Huh. I've never heard of such a thing."

She shrugged. "The truth is, after last night, I feel like I'm more your wife than I ever was his."

Dalton nodded, kissed her softly and gathered their various papers and identification without further comment on her first marriage. "Then let's make this official."

Once it was their turn in line, they opted for a no-frills standard wedding package. They didn't have flowers, although he asked her twice to be sure she didn't want any. Dalton insisted on purchasing rings for them, including a very nice engagement ring, charging the entire service to his credit card. He purchased a trio of roses for his new bride—even though she never would have asked—making her very happy.

They drove away as Mr. and Mrs. Dalton Langston.

He had the final papers sent to a post office box in Lake Havasu, where they were headed for their "official" honeymoon.

Lina, seated alongside her husband of only one hour, felt more secure and happier about her future than she ever had in her life.

Dalton headed south, taking as many back roads out of Las Vegas as he could before hitting the main road to their destination.

The piece of shit car, or POS as he intended to refer to it from now on, was as expected, shitty. The ride was rough and the engine sluggish, but at least they were out of town.

Lina was quiet. After watching her for a few minutes, it occurred to him that she probably hadn't slept at all since their lustful lovemaking.

"How long will it take to get there?" She yawned, hiding her mouth behind the back of the hand that sported his ring.

"A couple of hours. Maybe you should get some shuteye."

"I might take a nap. I haven't really slept yet since..." She stopped talking, glanced in his direction, and continued softly with, "...well, since what happened last night."

"Go ahead and rest. I slept like the dead for a few hours right after we showered and snuggled in bed."

"Is that why you married me? Because of last night?"

"No. Well, it didn't hurt. I married you because you asked me. But I wouldn't have married you if I didn't have feelings for you. That's why I jumped at the chance and said yes. From a practical perspective, I understand that you want protection and I want to provide it for you.

This way if your parents do show up or send someone to get you, it won't matter. You can't be married off to anyone of their choosing again."

"Especially once the marriage has been consummated," she added. "I know that means we have to have sex again, technically. Believe me, I can't wait." She yawned again. "I need a nap first, though."

"I know timing is everything, and trust me, I want to have sex with you again, too, but since we had sex less than twelve hours before getting married, maybe it already counts. Either way, no one can force you to marry another man. You're mine."

"Am I?"

Dalton looked at her sleepy features, falling even more for her innocent expression. Each moment he spent in her presence made him feel like he'd done the best thing he ever could have in the suitable partner department. Maybe he wasn't falling for his new bride. Maybe he was already in love with her. "Yes. You were a virgin our first time and that makes you mine."

"Is that why you married me, then? Because you were the first man in my bed? Is this some sort of honorable intention you felt the need to bear?"

"As I said, I married you because you asked me to. I married you because it helps protect you from your parents' horrific matrimonial plans. I also married you because I'm falling in love with you. I have been since I only saw a black and white bus station photo and thought you looked very familiar. And you were, as it turned out."

Her mouth dropped open and then she smiled. "Maybe I'm falling in love with you, too. I haven't forgotten three months' worth of dreams about your incredible backside."

He laughed out loud. "Thanks. I like your backside, too."

"Then we're perfect for each other."

Dalton nodded. "Get some sleep, bride of mine. Most importantly, you're safe. In fact, we're both safe. You can relax."

She leaned her seat way back and curled up on her side, facing him. She was completely adorable. His wife. His beautiful, feisty wife. He spent more time looking down at her sleeping than he did looking at the road or perhaps it had been equal time.

Lina didn't move at all, even when he pulled into the parking area by his small trailer at the Coyote Willow campground and stopped the car. Opening the driver's door didn't disturb her either.

Dalton walked around to the far side of the trailer and grabbed the spare key. Alex and his future wife Veronica had been here most recently. He'd been assured they'd washed the sheets and cleaned up before heading out, even leaving behind some food in trade for the safe place to stay.

He grabbed the key from the hiding place near the water turn-on switch, flipped the switch on and unlocked the trailer door and set the air conditioner to automatically come on when the temperature rose. When he returned to the car, Lina was still sound asleep in her seat.

Dalton opened her door, unbuckled her seatbelt, carefully extracted her from the front seat and carried her to the partly open trailer door. She wrapped her arms around his neck and buried her face at his throat, whispering, "You smell good," before sagging in his arms again without ever opening her eyes. He'd obviously married Sleeping Beauty. He was a lucky man.

He negotiated them up three steps and through the narrow door without dropping her on her head, which was truly a miracle. It was tradition that he carried her across the threshold of his domain. Too bad she was sound asleep and didn't realize it. He deposited his new bride on top of the neatly made bed at the back of the trailer. She slept on blissfully.

Checking for supplies, Dalton noted his brother had left him enough food for a few simple meals before they would need to head into town. He went back outside to grab Lina's bags out of the car, locking it up before returning.

He also called a friend from The Organization to pick up his car at the bus station in Vegas and drive it back to Ironwood. Luckily, he kept a spare key hidden in the wheel well.

Dalton put Lina's things on the small dining room table. He glanced at Lina. She hadn't moved. Smiling at her adorable fatigue, Dalton decided to join her. He dumped everything out of his pockets—keys, wallet, phone and loose change—placing it on the table next to her things.

He then kicked his boots off and removed his socks. He peeled his clothing off slowly down to his boxer briefs, then took the time to remove her shoes, socks, T-shirt and jeans, all the while expecting her to wake up. She only sighed a couple of times as if in pure contentment.

Dalton crawled on top of the comforter alongside his new bride, kissing the back of her neck and snuggling up behind her to get some long-needed sleep as dawn broke fully in the Eastern sky and the sun rose well above the skyline.

They both woke up later to full morning sun shining through the windows and the sound of his phone vibrating on top of his rattling loose change. The ringing stopped, but started up again. Someone was impatient to get hold of him.

"What time is it?" she asked in a sleepy sweet voice he wanted to eat up with a spoon.

"Don't know. Let me check." He scooted off the bed and padded over to his phone, noting it was a bit after nine in the morning. The phone had stopped again, but seconds later a third call buzzed, putting him in a foul mood. Snatching up his phone, Dalton practically roared, "What?"

Ivan Dragovic's voice came through the line. "Did you get the rest of the money?" he asked in an equally harsh voice. "Please tell me you are already out hunting down my daughter."

Fuck.

CHAPTER 13

Lina woke in a strange place, unable to remember how she'd gotten here. She opened her eyes as Dalton slid out of the bed they were in. At first glance it looked like a small travel trailer. Opening her eyes wider confirmed it.

How had she gotten from the car to the bed? She didn't remember. She looked down at her body and realized most of her clothes were missing and she had no memory of that happening either. It was a bit unsettling, but not as much as the look on Dalton's face when he answered his phone.

Wide-eyed and somber, Dalton turned his back on her to speak into the phone in a low tone. She didn't know what the conversation was about, as she hadn't heard the first part of it, but Dalton kept saying, "No. I'm afraid this isn't going to work out. No. I'm still not interested at a higher rate." He repeated it several times along with, "No. Still not interested. Please go elsewhere." He said some other things as well, but in a tone too low for her to hear.

The muted conversation didn't last long, but also obviously didn't end with either party very happy or satisfied. Had the call been from her father? She hoped not. Then again, it sounded like Dalton had turned down a job. Maybe she did hope it was her father's call he turned down.

Dalton made another phone call soon after hanging up, but apparently didn't get through, because he left a two-word message of, "Call me," and tossed his phone back on the pile of loose change. Then he smiled at her and returned to bed.

"Good morning, Mrs. Langston," he said and kissed her cheek.

Her gaze shot to the third finger of her left hand and registered the weight of the rings he'd put on her finger only hours before.

"We're married." The words came out as a statement, not a question.

"That's right," Dalton said, moving close and kissing her neck. "Is it time for our honeymoon, yet?"

"Perhaps."

"That doesn't sound promising."

"Honestly, I'm not certain I'm awake enough yet."

He laughed. "I'm not either. Let's discuss this after we've slept more than a couple of hours in a row."

"Perfect." She wanted to ask him if the call had been from her father, but she was too tired to form the question. She also wasn't certain she wanted to know what the result of the conversation had been. When her father found out she was married, there might be hell to pay.

Lina put her head on Dalton's shoulder, draped an arm over his chest and put her bent leg over his thigh, feeling very possessive of this man. He was hers. She had the papers to prove it. She inhaled his masculine scent with a hint of cologne. It made him nearly irresistible.

They hadn't discussed the length of this marriage going forward into their uncertain future. Even though he'd told her he cared for her, this union was not intended to last forever, was it? Perhaps once her father found out he'd derail any future plans they made, but she hoped not. She hoped this marriage kept her safe because it would be very easy to fall in love with Dalton and never look back.

She wished for that very thing. To be in love with and married to a man who was protective of her, knew her well enough to track her down repeatedly and most of all hadn't betrayed her to ensure his own gains was refreshing. And sexy. Maybe he could love her, too. He said he was falling in love with her. Was he sincere? She chose to believe he meant it as she drifted back into dreamland.

Lina was in and out of sleep for the next few hours. The sunlight remained bright throughout the small trailer. She didn't know how long she rested, but woke still attached to Dalton like she was part of him.

She wanted to be even closer. A very bold thought occurred to her when she noticed that Dalton's cock was semi-rigid and wedged beneath her knee. What if she climbed on top of him and woke him up with their first sex since getting married?

He slept soundly on his back, not moving when she stealthily pulled his underwear down to release the spectacular part of his anatomy she wanted to enjoy. He also didn't wake when she removed her panties and bra and climbed on top of him. His lids fluttered as if he tried to wake, but hadn't quite accomplished it yet.

Before her new husband woke up completely, Lina wrapped her hand around his stiffness, stroking him a few times as he moaned in his sleep. She took this as encouragement and shifted her hips so she could impale herself on him. Once she started riding him, she expected he'd wake up soon enough.

And he did.

She drove her body down over his wide, satisfying erection. In a second, Dalton came up on his elbows with a decidedly sexy groan.

"That feels way too good," he said in a gravely tone, like sex on a stick. It only served to make her want him more.

"I agree," she said a bit breathlessly. Lina sped up her motions, moving her hips up and down, faster and faster. The friction and her position rubbed her hot spot exactly the right way each time she impaled herself with gusto.

Dalton reached for her, placing a hand at the base of her spine. He also drew her mouth down to his, kissing her as if with sincere desperation. She started rotating her hips a bit as she drove her body down over his, trying to stroke herself in the perfect place for her own gratification.

Lina was so close to flying over the edge of a pleasurable abyss she sped her movements, searching for release. Dalton thrust upward beneath her, making the perfect contact, ensuring her ultimate satisfaction was now imminent.

Three more solid drives of his rising hips and pleasure burst from where they were intimately connected, pulsing up through her body like a geyser. The scream she let loose was from the depths of her soul. The sound of her delight reverberated along the low ceiling above the bed and into the cabin behind them.

Dalton grunted beneath her, thrusting harder, faster, deeper as she felt every inch of him penetrating her body. The rush almost brought on a second wave of ecstasy. Her lips went numb. She felt a little faint, but it felt so good she held on for the rest of the ride.

After only a few more powerful strokes, Dalton growled like a gratified beast. His hand gripped one hip as if he wanted to meld their bodies together permanently.

A warm sensation filled her the moment he stiffened. They were held in exquisite sexual captivation for a count of three. He soon relaxed against the covers, breathing hard. One hand still pressed hard against her lower back. All five of his large fingers pushed firmly into her flesh, like he'd claimed her forever, refusing to stop touching her.

A smile surfaced at the idea of being Dalton's forever.

She was out of breath, too, slumping forward to rest her head on his shoulder.

"That was the best," she said. "Is it different because we're married now?"

Dalton shook his head. "I don't know about that, but I know for a fact it was spectacular for me because we didn't use a condom this time." He continued breathing hard as a flash of equal parts panic and elation tried to claim ground in her mind.

No condom. She was so foolish. What if she got pregnant? Even more foolish delight grew within her soul. If she was pregnant with the child of a man her parents didn't approve of, maybe she was saved. Maybe her parents would disown her. Maybe she'd never have to worry about going back home. Maybe she could have a child with a man she loved.

Lina looked into Dalton's intense gaze as another thought occurred. What if Dalton was angry with her for possibly getting pregnant?

Dalton was so relaxed from their most recent bout of phenomenal sex he hardly knew what to do. Yes, it was foolish to have sex without a condom. No, he didn't regret it for a single second.

The sensation of lovemaking without a barrier was

clearly the pinnacle of his previous sexual experiences. He'd never gone without protection before, ever. But then he worried that she might be upset.

He'd agreed to marry her to protect her from her scheming parents and to give her choices about her future. Getting her pregnant the first day they were married likely wasn't in her plans, but he found it difficult not to smile deep inside at the prospect of fatherhood.

His brother Reece had twins, a boy and a girl who were less than a year old and they were very cute little tykes. Just thinking about his sweet niece and nephew brought a sincere smile to his soul.

Without warning, the recent phone call from her father intruded on his jubilant mood. Even a few minutes of talking to Lina's father had left a bad taste in his mouth.

Ivan Dragovic had been wholly unreasonable about not getting his way with regard to hiring Dalton to hunt down his daughter, as he'd so eloquently put it. Like Lina was a wild animal needing a cage or a tamer. She didn't need either. Dragovic had threatened all manner of dire things mostly related to Dalton's never working again as a bounty hunter. Dalton had a position with The Organization. Bounty hunter was simply a side gig for those phone calls from people without the capacity to take no for an answer, like Dragovic, ironically enough.

"Are you angry with me?" Lina whispered in a very serious tone.

His eyes had closed and he might have drifted a bit before her question surprised him back awake.

"No." Dalton tried to dismiss her father's call and any ramifications he and Lina might have to look forward to in the short term—hopefully none—from his thoughts. Even so, he decided against mentioning it to Lina for now. Her worried expression drew all his attention.

"I'm so sorry about forgetting the protection. I just

woke all tangled up next to you and I didn't think through everything."

Dalton put a hand on her cheek, stroking her soft skin gently to reassure her. "It's more my fault than yours."

She kissed his palm, making it tingle. "It is?"

"Yes. You're new to this and I'm not. Even so, apparently I wasn't awake enough to stop you. Besides, it felt too fucking good to stop and I probably wouldn't have anyway."

"I agree."

"Do you?" She nodded sedately, a smile playing over her lips. Dalton tucked one arm behind his head, staring at his beautiful bride. He tucked a stray strand of hair behind her ear.

In a soulful whisper, he asked, "Would you say that for me?"

"What?"

"The exact words I just said before about how it felt." He didn't remember hearing her use any curse words since they'd met. Was it wrong to want to hear her say the word "fuck"?

A small smile tugged at the corner of her mouth. "So you want me to say, 'It felt too *fucking* good to stop,' is that right?" she asked in a soft, sultry voice that made his balls tighten the moment she swore.

"Yes, I really do." He was delighted by her question and the way she emphasized the word "fucking" in her query.

"Okay." Her expression was sublime. In a lower and even more seductive tone, she said slowly and carefully, "Dalton, having sex with you without a condom in place felt too *fucking* good to stop."

Dalton's mouth opened slightly in immediate response, even though it was the second time she'd said it. He stared at her without responding.

"Was that good? Was it the way you wanted to hear

it?" A full-blown smile surfaced as her cheeks filled with color.

He laughed out loud and hugged her close. "It was perfect. Both times. Thank you."

"Whatever. Men seem to enjoy the most foolish things."

"Perhaps you're right. But I think that's the first time I've ever heard you say the F-word."

"It's not like I've never heard the word 'fuck' before since living in Las Vegas. Especially considering the first roommate I had."

"Oh, yeah? How so? Was your roommate a sailor?"

"No. She was an exotic dancer. Her name was Roberta and she lived a rather exuberant lifestyle with sex as the main component. She'd bring a different guy home every single weekend—sometimes one man on Friday night and a different guy on Saturday. Anyway, the F-word was used repeatedly and in various ways as she consummated her quick and often onetime relationships."

"Such as?" Dalton prompted her. When her brows narrowed as if puzzled, he added, "Give me an example or two of how she used it."

Lina looked up at the ceiling as if trying to recall a memory. "For example, '*Fuck* me, you feel so *fucking* good.' Sometimes she'd insert the guy's name, '*Fuck* me, name of new man, you feel so *fucking* good,' but mostly just the generic phrase. I don't think she ever cared to know their names."

Dalton laughed. "Is that all?"

"Oh no. Another favorite expletive during her sexual exploits was simply, '*Fuck, fuck, fuck, fuck*,' grunted and growled over and over again as they...well, fucked like bunnies."

"But you never found a guy to make noises or say the F-word with?"

She shook her head, looking a bit sad.

"Why not?"

A small shrug. "I was trying to be low key. I didn't want anyone to find me or take pictures of me or put me out on social media or try to get involved with me when I was doing my best to hide. I wanted to be invisible and to my way of thinking, invisible meant being alone."

"I never found any social media information on you before you left home," Dalton said.

"My parents are firmly entrenched in last-century values. They did not want me or their business available online in any manner for the world to see. But I knew if they hired someone professional, any and all tools would be used to find me. I was afraid of letting myself get interested in anyone for fear of being tracked down. If I'd known you and your bloodhound skills existed, perhaps I wouldn't have bothered. I was desperate. I likely would have tried to disappear regardless."

"Regrets?" he asked.

She shrugged again, but then caught his gaze. "No, not really, although if I'd known how amazing sex was, I might have reconsidered my options."

"Oh? Will I have to keep my eye on you?"

"No. The truth is that I was never tempted by anyone else. At least not until you came back."

"Lucky me." Dalton meant it, too. He should have come back to find her sooner. If he hadn't been so busy working for The Organization the last few months, he would have. He'd thought about the girl with the long dark hair more than once after chasing that idiot bond jumper through the casino. Shortly after that, he'd gone undercover for a couple of months, returning in time to help his brother Alex.

From time to time, he'd think back to Las Vegas and the girl he'd wanted to talk to, but instead got sidetracked when his mark finally showed up. Inconvenient bastard.

If he were completely honest, he'd tell her she was the reason he was even in Nevada. Wasn't she why he'd come to Las Vegas to start his vacation when he could have gone absolutely anywhere else in the world?

Hadn't he secretly hoped to find the dark-haired girl from the restaurant and finally ask her out, which had been his intention the first time he'd approached her?

Destiny had put her in his path so that now, on day two of his vacation, she was his blushing bride. It was either totally random and crazy or fated and meant to be. He voted for the latter.

"I must tell you that I feel like the lucky one." Lina kissed his mouth gently and Dalton pretty much forgot everything in his head.

He kissed her in return, hugging her close, rolling her onto her back until she was beneath him and he could move within her warm, slick body once more. They'd never completely disengaged and now he didn't want to.

Dalton grew steadily within her silken folds as they kissed and kissed and kissed some more. She clung to him, widening her legs and even wrapping one ankle around the back of his thigh to make it easier for him to thrust slowly inside her tight, warm body as his cock thickened.

He was addicted to the way he felt when they were as close as two people could be. He was addicted to the way she made him feel when they merely talked to each other. He was addicted to having sex with his beautiful, feisty, clever bride and knew he'd move heaven and earth to make her happy, regardless of this being more of a marriage of convenience. As far as he was concerned, it could be convenient for the rest of their lives.

She arched in his arms, breaking their exuberant kiss. He trailed kisses down her throat until he crested the top of one breast, clamping his lips around her nipple to her further cries of encouragement.

One hand was fastened to her lower spine, pulling her into each of his ferociously deep thrusts. He pushed his other hand between them to stroke her clit and ensure she had a shattering climax like he was about to experience.

Half a dozen firm brushes across her sensitive nub was all it took for her to come apart in his arms. She groaned, then she screamed, then she moaned and screamed at the same time. Her already tight sheath squeezed his shaft rhythmically to his utter fucking delight.

Dalton sucked her nipple, thrust his cock deeply into her taut warm body and came in a hard rush of pleasure the likes of which he'd never, ever experienced before.

The cataclysmic release centered in his lower half, spewing a satisfying buzzing sensation to his limbs, to his heart, to his very soul. He wanted to suspend them both in this very instant of time and go back to relive it again and again.

He momentarily forgot how to breathe, his vision going a little dark and wavy around the edges, even though his eyes were already closed. A sound much like a satisfied beast exited his lips, roaring his approval to the heavens before he collapsed on top of her, spent and useless and finally spurring his lungs to take in air again.

In his ear, he heard Lina, also out of breath, whispering, "So amazing. So *fucking* amazing, my love." His internal joy pinged at the top of the scale. Everything she did made him fall just a little harder for her.

He clenched her tight in his arms, kissed her hard on the mouth, and shifted their bodies so they were side by side so he wouldn't crush her when his strength gave out. It took sheer willpower to provide any movement at all.

Once on his side, Dalton buried his face in Lina's

throat and dropped into a deep, satisfied sleep, still intimately connected, still falling headlong and madly in love with his wife every second he spent with her.

He'd expected to marry only once in his lifetime. Perhaps his quick decision to marry Lina had been rash, but he didn't regret it. He'd searched for someone to make him feel the way she did.

Months ago and then days ago, she was still the only one who'd ever made his possibly foolish heart skip a beat with a mere look in his direction. If she wasn't his one and only and they parted, he'd die alone because he didn't want anyone else, ever.

CHAPTER 14

L ina stared at the top of Dalton's head, reaching out to smooth his ruffled dark blond hair into place. He was seriously a very attractive man, at least in her possibly biased opinion. He didn't move, didn't wake up and didn't open his eyes no matter where she touched him.

She ran her fingertips from his forearm to his shoulder, stopping briefly at his prominent biceps, marveling at his beautiful muscles. He was strong. He was tall. He was funny and considerate and sweet. He was amazing in bed. And best of all he was hers. A smile shaped her lips without conscience effort every time she remembered that fact.

Her only worry was his thoughts on what the length of this marriage might be. He'd mentioned falling in love with her, but they hadn't spoken about the duration of this spontaneous wedding. Even if he loved her or felt honor bound to marry her out of respect for being her first lover, feelings could change. If her parents left her alone or let her go to do what she wanted with her life because of this drive-through wedding, would Dalton also want his freedom from her eventually?

So far he seemed very interested, but perhaps it was

because they were literally in the honeymoon phase of their relationship. How many times had she heard of couples spending the first few days in exuberant joy after meeting and hastily marrying in Sin City, only to sit staring at each other with sullen contempt by the end of a two-week vacation and about to return to the reality of two lives that would never co-exist very well, if at all? The obvious answer was too many times to believe her drive-through marriage of convenience would be any different, but she wasn't ready to deal with that worry now.

Lina decided not to borrow trouble until she was forced to manage whatever reality was in store for her...much later, if she had any input.

The tiny, romantic part of her would be devastated to lose him, but she'd get over it. Eventually. She was practical enough to know forever was often not truly an option, regardless of her feelings. She stared down at her new husband, enjoying the view for the time being.

Dalton slept solidly, not waking or even breaking the rhythm of his breathing when she pulled away to clean up in the trailer's tiny bathroom. She gathered her clothing from the floor and the edge of the bed, something else she didn't remember happening, but smiled at the notion her husband had undressed her before putting her to bed.

When she emerged from the bathroom several minutes later feeling fresher and more awake, Dalton hadn't moved a single whisker. She decided to let him sleep.

Lina crept down the short hall, exploring the small trailer she'd apparently been carried into when they arrived. A careful search yielded a single-cup coffee brewer and the plastic pods to make a very strong cup of coffee, just the way she liked it.

She also preferred a bit of sugar or sweetener to take

the bitter edge off, but didn't see any after searching all the cupboards as quietly as she could.

Instead, Lina found several cans of soup and a box of crackers. They wouldn't starve in the immediate future. She also found a mostly full jar of peanut butter. She was dubious it could still be fresh enough to eat, but the expiration date was more than a year away and it smelled delicious when she unscrewed the lid to do a sniff test.

She also dipped her finger into the jar and scooped out a good-sized amount for a taste test before replacing the lid and licking her finger clean. Her stomach gurgled in gratitude.

She sat at the small dining table, which held all of her bags, thankful her husband had been thoughtful enough to bring them in from the car. Lina might have panicked a bit without being able to check her backpack for her few valuables.

After looking through her things and finding everything in place, Lina searched the rest of the trailer, searching for something to do.

In the driver's seatback she found someone had stuffed a crossword puzzle book complete with a pencil in the fold. She pulled it out, and flattened it with the intent of occupying herself until Dalton woke up. In the same place, she saw the corner of a battered envelope jutting up. She pulled it out carefully, glancing at the bed to ensure Dalton still slept. She felt like she was intruding on his privacy, but not enough to put the envelope back.

She lifted the flap and pulled out a stack of pictures. The one on top had a picture of five very attractive men, all arm in arm, grinning at the camera. One was Dalton, and she suspected that since they all looked so similar, these were his brothers. Five boys. Wow.

Several names were written on the back of the photo

in careful block letters. Alex. Reece. Zak. Deke. Dalton. Key West, dated October a few years ago. She flipped through several more photos showcasing different combinations of the same five guys and with the same careful printing on the back of each picture.

The very last picture included their parents. They looked like a very happy family. Lina's eyes watered up. She wished her family had been as fun as these pictures represented. She wouldn't say she'd had a bad childhood, but it was vastly different from that of other families she'd gotten to know before and after leaving home.

Petra was her best friend and like a sister. She'd always made Lina feel welcome and like she was part of her family, just as Petra's brother and parents had done. While they were not poor, Petra's family wasn't quite in the same elite class as Lina's. At least that's what her mother always told her.

"Don't get too attached, Nikolina," her mother warned. "It's fine for now, but once you marry, you won't be in the same social circles."

Lina had always wanted to tell her mother she'd rather stay in Petra's social circle, as it was more enjoyable, but knew her mother wouldn't understand. Fun wasn't something to be sought in life, according to her parents' philosophy. Money was the only thing she was taught to chase. Money was all.

In the back of the envelope was a picture of Dalton with a beautiful redhead in a bikini. They were both grinning wildly in the photo and in the background was a pool and what looked to be in a tropical setting.

A shocking streak of jealousy raced through her body, putting Lina in a sullen mood the moment she registered what the photo displayed. Dalton happy and hugged up to a very beautiful woman was a horrid punch to her soul. She couldn't be his sister. He said he didn't have any sisters.

She flipped the picture over to read the careful block letters that identified the people in the photo. Dalton and Veronica, Key West, but no date was listed as to when it had been taken. Last week, last month, last century—there was no way to know.

Lina turned the photo over and studied it more closely, finding something even worse. *Veronica* wore a very lovely engagement ring with a huge diamond. Was this a woman Dalton had once been engaged to? Was he still engaged to her? Why weren't they married? Why had he kept the picture? Why didn't it have a date like the others?

The very idea that Dalton could have been in love with and engaged to someone else, especially this smiling redheaded beauty, made Lina instantly despondent. From across the trailer, she heard Dalton stir, as if her interior tantrum had somehow mentally signaled him from a distance.

She wiped foolish tears from her eyes with the backs of her fingers. With one last glance at the image of Dalton and Veronica, Lina quickly stuffed all the photos back into the envelope. She folded the flap in place, turned in her seat, and shoved the now offending packet of photos into the driver's seatback pocket.

She whipped back around, grabbed the pencil and pretended to work on a crossword puzzle. From the bed, she heard Dalton stir a bit more until he called out, "Lina?"

She was grateful he'd said *her* name and not Veronica's. Lina shook her head at herself. No. She would not stoop to petty jealousy. Maybe it was only a family friend. *Sure, also unicorns really exist and love always ends with a big happily ever after scene.* Reality was a cold *fucking* bitch.

Her eyes were scratchy and suddenly irritated. Lina carefully rubbed her lids, and realized she still wore her blue contact lenses. No wonder her eyes felt so sensitive. They didn't offer anything in the way of corrective vision. They were merely vanity lenses to change her eye color so she could hide more effectively.

Dalton stirred again, half sitting up in bed although he didn't look in her direction. "Lina, are you here?" He didn't sound in the least awake.

"Yes. Go back to sleep," she called out. She wanted to add that she'd join him soon, but pressed her lips together to keep from speaking. Sadness welled up inside her throat, threatening to spill out and display her feelings. He didn't need to hear them. She needed more time to sort out her feelings.

Dalton slid back onto his stomach, flattening himself on the bed. He murmured something she didn't hear, but he didn't talk again or get up.

Lina reached for her backpack and the case she kept her blue contacts in when she wasn't wearing them. With the challenge of no mirror, she managed to remove them and deposit each lens in the case with saline solution, screwing the lids on tight and returning it all to her backpack.

Now that they were legally married, albeit Vegas style in a drive-through chapel, and regardless of any other women in Dalton's life, she didn't need to hide any longer.

If her parents found her, she had a marriage document with Dalton proving they couldn't marry her off to anyone else. Her only concern was putting Dalton's life in the crosshairs of her family's greed, hoping they wouldn't have any options with regard to her life going forward.

There was still the possibility of annulment, but since they'd been intimate, a dissolution would be more difficult for her parents to demand, especially since she and Dalton had foregone a condom most recently.

Twice. Ironically, her life would certainly be her own if she carried a child. The vision of a baby with Dalton's features registered briefly, and the idea of it didn't dismay her.

But then a horrifyingly morose thought occurred. What if she did get pregnant, but discovered Dalton loved another? Maybe he and Veronica weren't still engaged. But what if he loved the redhead more than he cared about Lina and being her first lover?

She'd asked—well, demanded—that they get married, and he agreed, but maybe he only intended their marriage to be temporary. What if he wanted to get an annulment after she was safe because he wanted to woo Veronica back?

Lina—suddenly filled with crushing self-doubt—wanted Dalton to love her, but perhaps she was deluding herself. She'd have to pull her head out of the clouds, remove her heart from her sleeve and realize Dalton had done her a favor. That was all.

By marrying her and giving her an opportunity to change the direction of her life, he kept her from whatever her parents' current greedy plans entailed. But that didn't mean he intended for their marriage to be forever. Of course he didn't. Why would he? When he'd told her he was falling in love with her, it was in the rush of the moment. Perhaps he'd regret those words later. Perhaps in a month they'd be seated in a café, Dalton staring sullenly at her and wishing they weren't tied together, admitting his true feelings for an old flame, Veronica, to get rid of his unwanted wife.

Anguish rose quickly and she had to swallow hard to keep from sobbing out loud. She glanced at Dalton's beautiful form.

Lina wasn't sure why he'd married her if he had a gorgeous redhead named Veronica waiting for him. But she promised to be grateful when he woke up. The marriage being consummated was the one detail she clung to in order to keep her parents at bay. The melty part of her heart seized a little as memories of their lovemaking intruded, but she batted her foolish lovesick ideas back into place.

He'd seemed enthralled during their exuberant sexual activities, but so had every one of Roberta's lovers, until the weekend was over and they were never seen or heard from again.

Lina needed to be practical. Dalton had never promised her forever. Not exactly, anyway. Their quickie wedding vows had said something along those lines, but she shook off any sentimentality. Their marriage was for a specific purpose. She had told him the only way she'd feel safe was for him to marry her. He'd agreed readily enough, but that didn't mean he intended for them to be together forever.

Of course he didn't. Why would he? Especially if there was a redheaded girl named Veronica in his life, possibly waiting for him in the tropical location by the pool.

Yes, it hurt. Yes, she was a fool. Yes, she'd been busy falling in love with him since the first time they'd met three months ago. And, yes, every thought since they'd been together these past couple of whirlwind days always included the two of them together in a perfect future. However, that foolish dream had been swept away by a single photograph. Every photograph might be worth a thousand words, but Lina hadn't needed that many to understand the abrupt change her life might take.

In this moment, Lina truly missed Petra. No matter what happened when she lived with her parents, Lina could always count on Petra to say the exact perfect thing to cheer her up and make her life seem not so bad. She hadn't spoken to or heard from Petra in months.

What would Petra say about her drive-through wedding? Lina smiled.

Petra, she knew, would be enamored of not only the unique way she'd gotten married, she'd also drool over her new, tall, handsome husband and tell Lina to keep him at all costs.

Further, she'd dismiss the photo of the redheaded beauty as not at all important or insist the woman was a cousin in order to make Lina smile again. Ever the romantic optimist, Petra was a gem. A true friend. A friend she missed, bringing more tears to her scratchy eyes. Lina desperately wanted to hear Petra's voice.

Lina shouldn't try to contact her. There had been several times over the last few months when she'd had a finger poised over a phone, ready to take a chance and dial just so she could hear her friend's voice. But she'd always been too afraid to go through with it.

Right this moment, she didn't think she could talk herself out of a call to her friend. And if she heard Petra's voice, she'd be unable to simply hang up without talking to her, or rather, spill every detail of her current situation with Dalton.

Even though she was safely married to Dalton for the time being, if she ever needed a friend to talk to it was right exactly now. Glancing at the door, she fought the urge to take a walk and find a phone to use. If any pay phones still existed in the area, it would offer her some protection. Should she take the chance? Probably not.

She did have a backup for this purpose, but it was a onetime mechanism. Should she use it now? Was this situation truly dire? No, it wasn't.

Once Dalton woke up, Lina intended to discuss their future in great detail along with setting a specific date when they would part. Forever.

CHAPTER 15

Dalton roused alone in bed on his belly after sleeping for he didn't even know how long. He was so relaxed from the recent and quite amazing sexual activities that it took a few more minutes to get his verbal skills to work. He rose up a few inches on his elbows, with his eyes still closed.

"Lina?" he called out. "Are you here?"

"Yes. Go back to sleep." She sounded like she was over by the dining table.

Good, he thought, slumping easily back to his original sleeping pose of flat on his face. He loved married life. No wonder his brothers had raced down the aisle to attain wives. Marriage was amazing.

If only he got to keep her. That depressing thought rolled around in his head for a few seconds. Maybe he'd married her too quickly and on a whim, with the initial intent of giving her better life choices, but now that they'd officially consummated their quickie Vegas elopement, he wanted more.

Dalton dozed off thinking about the next Key West gathering with his parents, his brothers and their wives. Now he had a wife to take there, too. He'd acquired an awesome plus one and best of all he didn't need to dodge any female family members' attempts to set him up with strange women. Win-win.

He stretched, trying in earnest to wake up and get motivated. His stomach growled. The last meal he'd had, he'd shared with Lina. It ended with an amazing dessert right after they'd split cherry pie and chocolate cake.

"Lina?" he said, expecting her to respond like she had last time.

Nothing.

Dalton sat up in bed, visually searching every nook and cranny of the small trailer to find he was all alone. He tapped his knuckle lightly on the wall where the tiny bathroom was located.

Nothing.

He scrubbed both hands up and down his face to fend off the lethargy, scooted off the bed and retrieved his clothing, still piled in the same place he'd left it before getting into bed. He dressed quickly, starting to get concerned about Lina's whereabouts.

Glancing out the window, he saw the rental POS parked where he'd left it, but the view didn't afford much else. The car keys were on the table next to his wallet and phone, seemingly undisturbed.

Lina's clothes were gone from where he'd dropped them after putting her to bed, but her bags were still on the dining table, including her precious backpack. There was a crossword puzzle flattened on the table. Where had that come from?

Dalton grabbed all of his stuff, pocketing it quickly, and exited the trailer. The day was warm even for this time of year. He closed the door and walked to the camp's public bathroom to use the facilities, as his trailer was cramped and difficult on a good day to accommodate his height.

He loitered around the ladies' room briefly, listening for Lina, but didn't see her or hear anyone else inside, for that matter. Searching the area from this vantage didn't yield any obvious destinations. The only other place she might possibly go was the camp office.

Once he rounded the far side of the bathroom, he saw the corner of the building and the camp flag waving in the breeze. It depicted a coyote next to what he assumed was a willow tree. He started walking in that direction, remembering that there was a small convenience store inside. His stomach made another unruly noise.

Maybe her tummy had also growled and she went in search of food. He often relied on his gut, hungry or not, to determine possible data and how to act on certain information. He didn't have a bad feeling—at least not yet—but knew he'd feel much better once he laid eyes on his wife. Even thinking the word "wife" in relation to Lina gave Dalton a sappy and delighted feeling near his heart.

The high-pitched tinkle of a bell pealed over his head when he entered the camp office. On his right was the chest-high counter and the owner seated on a barstool behind it, pretending to read a magazine. Straight ahead was a small space devoted to snacks, drinks and the like with a waist-high counter. The owner's wife was seated in a chair behind it, pretending to do needlework.

Directly on his left was a small open area with several tables and chairs. He heard Lina's voice, more specifically her laughter, the moment the sound of the bell on the door exited his head.

Both of the owners were looking in her general direction, pretending not to listen in on her conversation. Which begged the questions, who was she talking to and what was she saying that so pegged their interest?

Dalton was still poised behind the door, so Lina couldn't see him, but the owner and his wife could. The look on their faces when they noticed him standing there told Dalton that perhaps Lina had been talking about him in her noisy private conversation with her mystery caller.

"Mr. Jones," the owner said loudly with a single nod in his direction. Dalton had always used this as a safe house to stow some of his bounties, so of course he hadn't put it under his real last name.

The owner's wife dropped her needlepoint the moment she heard his name, blushing and grabbing the fabric from the floor with a finger wave and an exuberant, "Nice to see you again, Mr. Jones!"

Lina didn't stop talking—she didn't know him as Mr. Jones. The sound of her candid laughter put him not only in a better mood, he also released the worried sigh he hadn't realized he held.

Dalton stepped through the door and turned to see his lovely wife talking on a cell phone he'd never seen before and seated at a table for two in the far corner of the room.

The door swung shut behind him and before he took a single step toward her table, her gaze shifted in his direction. Dalton was unprepared to see the utter panic she displayed at the sight of him.

She sucked in a deep breath. "Oh no. I've got to get off the phone, Petra." Her frown wasn't nearly as worrisome as the look of fear in her eyes. Her attention was momentarily drawn away as she tried to disengage the person on the other end of her phone call.

"No. I'm fine, truly." She flashed another worried look his way, turning back to her call. Her eyes slid shut and her lips pressed together as if in pain.

"No. Don't worry. I'll speak to you again soon." A pause ensued for a few seconds before her mouth trembled. She gave an obviously forced smile.

"Of course. I know you won't. I miss you, too. Bye, Petra." She pulled the phone away from her ear, folded it in half and promptly bent at the waist, shoving both hands between her legs like she'd assumed the crash position in a dicey airplane landing.

Elbows pressed to her knees, Lina didn't look at him when she said, "Are you angry?"

Dalton crossed the room and squatted before her. He put his hands on hers, pulling the phone from her light grasp.

"Where did you get the phone?"

She lifted her head, staring guiltily into his eyes. "I had it in my bag. It's a pre-paid cellular. I bought it early on as a one use item in case I needed it."

He nodded. "Why would I be angry? What did you do?"

She pushed out a long sigh. "I called someone I probably shouldn't have."

"Petra?" he asked. She flashed him a look of surprise and then must have realized she'd said her friend's name out loud.

"Yes, my friend from back home."

"Why would I be angry about that?"

Another guilty stare ensued before she shrugged, breaking the gaze to stare at the floor between them. "I haven't spoken to her since that night I ran away." She sniffed once or twice and Dalton was horrified to notice she'd been crying. What he could see of her eyes were red. She sniffed again.

"Wait," he said gazing at her intently. "Are your eyes a different color?"

She wiped her eyes for seemingly the thousandth time since removing her contacts. "Yes, your blue-eyed bride actually has brown eyes. Surprise. I wore contacts to help hide my identity."

His lazy grin seemed to surprise her. "I like your brown eyes, bride of mine."

"Thank you."

"Why am I supposed to be mad?"

"I know we are on the run and hiding out. I shouldn't have made the call. I know it. But I was just so—" She stopped talking abruptly, her cheeks filling with color.

"You were just so what?"

"Lonely." Her puffy-eyed gaze lifted to his again. "I was lonesome and in need of a friend to talk to." She hadn't touched him since he got close, pulling her hands away after he took the phone.

Dalton narrowed his eyes, wondering what the holy hell he'd done to make her cower around him. "I don't understand what has happened since the last time we spoke to make you feel so lonely that you needed to phone a friend."

"I discovered...well...sort of found...and I thought that—" She stopped stuttering and shook her head, sniffing a few times as if trying to get hold of her volatile emotions. He didn't have a clue what was wrong.

Dalton leaned close. Her luscious scent slammed into his lungs the nearer he got. He stroked his hand from the top of her head to her shoulder, kissing her cheek gently, trying to figure out what had so upset her and why she didn't want to talk to him about it.

"You can tell me."

She shook her head gently. "I don't want to talk about it."

"Please tell me. What did you find, Lina?"

"Her." A sob escaped. "I found a picture of you and a woman together."

"A woman?" he asked, sounding like he'd never heard the word before.

"Yes. A beautiful redhead with her arm wrapped around you. Your fiancée, I presume."

Lina was completely miserable. She was in love with a man who was engaged to another woman. That was exactly the kind of luck she expected to have of late.

Believing her marriage was a temporary sham on both sides of the equation had finally prompted her to make a phone call to her friend. She shouldn't have chanced making the call, given that her family was still on the hunt for her.

She was afraid that even their legal drive-through marriage wouldn't keep her safe from her parents' ultimate plans. What if they coerced Dalton into divorcing her or annulling the marriage immediately?

The need to talk to her friend had become paramount, and regardless of what happened, Lina was delighted to talk to Petra.

"Fiancée?" he said, sounding very surprised by her knowledge. Well, she had been shocked, too.

Dalton cleared his throat and whispered, "Could we resume this conversation back in our trailer?"

Lina looked up and saw the owner and his wife staring in their direction. They didn't even make a pretense of reading or sewing anymore, just stared at them with prurient interest as if she and Dalton were a show at the circus.

She'd created the drama for these people to watch. And she knew better after a lifetime of learning not to draw unwanted attention. Not only was she hopelessly in love with her husband, she'd endangered them by calling her friend and made an additional spectacle of the situation by allowing strangers to listen in on sensitive information. She was overwrought.

"I'm so sorry," she whispered miserably. She had never been a girl who cried much, but currently, she was on the edge of an epic sob-fest.

She turned to him and he kissed her. Not a peck on the lips to make it look good for an audience, but a deep, sensuous, tongue-tangling kiss that knocked her socks into the next state. She heard a moan and realized she'd made the sexy noise.

Dalton broke the kiss, grinned like a man who knew he'd satisfied his woman and helped her stand up. He gave her the phone, which was a surprise. She figured he'd break it in half and dispose of it. Instead, he took her hand, nodded at the owner and his wife once on their way out of the camp office, never uttering a word of blame or disapproval. He led her across the campground to their trailer, opened the door and gestured for her to enter.

She might have balked, but he didn't seem to be the least bit angry. Not about the phone call. Not about the accusation of having another woman on the side. He seemed like the opposite of angry, like he was happy about something.

She seated herself at the dining table. Dalton sat across from her, folding his tall frame into the tight space.

Lina crossed her arms. Not in protection so much as defiance. She narrowed her gaze and said, "I think you are about to make fun of me."

A wide grin shaped his mouth. "No. I simply don't know where on earth you got the idea that I have a fiancée. Just so we are completely clear, I do not have any other woman in my life. Certainly not a fiancée with red hair. So why would you think that?"

She spun in her seat, grabbed the envelope of photos and pulled out the offending picture. She smashed it face up on the table. "This picture! This is the one that made me go off the deep end." Tears welled up in her eyes. "She's beautiful, of course. Why would you ever have an ugly fiancée? You wouldn't. What will she say when you tell her you married me, huh? What will you tell Veronica?"

"What makes you think she's my fiancée?"

She pointed to the engagement ring. The ring Lina wore that she hadn't even expected him to get for her before their quickie marriage was noticeably smaller. "The big fat diamond engagement ring she's wearing was my first clue. Will you even tell her about me, or maybe doesn't it matter because you plan to dump me as soon as possible? Did you plan to divorce me at your earliest convenience from the very beginning?"

Dalton studied the photos, picking up the envelope and pulling out the rest of the pictures and sorting through them until he found one and plucked it from the bunch. All five of his brothers were in it. "See this guy?"

Lina squinted, seeing one of his brothers. She didn't know which name went with the image. "Yes."

He picked up the photo with the redhead. "I'm not married to Veronica. My brother Alex is."

"Why are there a bunch of pictures with all five boys dated over the past several years and then only one of you and Veronica with no date on it? I don't see one of Veronica and Alex together. Why not?"

Dalton lifted one shoulder halfway and then dropped it. "I don't know. My mom sends me the pictures. I look at them, remember the last time we were together and then shove them in an envelope. There is another packet of pictures in a similar envelope back at my apartment in Ironwood. This picture was taken the day Alex asked Veronica to marry him."

"Then why are you in this picture and not Alex?"

Dalton grinned. "See how my clothes are all wet?"

She studied the photo. "Maybe." He was fully dressed and soaked to the bone. She hadn't noticed before now.

"Alex shoved me into the pool. When I crawled to the edge, heaving myself up, Veronica took pity and helped me climb out. Then my mom told us to pose and took our picture."

"Why did your brother shove you in the pool?"

He grinned. "I'm technically the youngest of five.

Usually there isn't a reason why any of them do anything to torture me. It just happens. Although as I recall, I may have made a remark Alex didn't like."

"Technically? You said that before. What does that even mean?"

He pointed to a different brother in the picture. "That's Deke. He's my twin brother."

"You have a twin?" She took the picture and looked at it closely. "Not identical."

"No. And technically he's ten minutes older."

Lina smiled and said, "You're taller though."

"Thank you. That's what I always say. However, I'm usually ignored."

Lina felt foolish to have embarrassed herself in this way. "Thank you for explaining."

"Do you believe me?"

She shrugged and then said, "Yes," in a very low tone.

"Are you sure?"

"Yes."

"Can we shake on it?" He held out his hand. She took it and he gripped her fingers tight. "Can we kiss on it, too?" He leaned forward.

She met him in the middle of the table. "Do you forgive me for being jealous?"

"Of course. Now I know you care."

"I do care. I'm sorry for jumping to the wrong conclusion."

Dalton nodded and a sly smile shaped his beautiful lips. "Do you think this might call for make up sex?"

Lina grinned. "Perhaps, but do you think we should keep tempting fate?"

One of his shoulders lifted halfway and dropped. "We're married. We can do anything we want."

"Even tempt fate?"

"Especially tempt fate."

"Do you want children?"

"Sure. Someday."

"Someday, but not now."

"If you get pregnant or you already are pregnant, I'm fine with that. If not, then maybe we could postpone parenthood and travel."

"Travel? Really?" She couldn't help but be excited about the prospect of going new places, as was her plan once she got the money her granny left her. "Where would we go?"

"Wherever you want. I've been to lots of beautiful places. I'd love to show them to you or take you to anywhere you've always wanted to go, or both."

Lina lit up inside with joy at the idea of her new husband—the one she didn't expect to keep—wanting to fulfill her fondest wish. "Do you truly mean that?"

He reached for her hand, squeezing it gently. "I do. I'll admit I have a deeply embedded sense of wanderlust."

"As I mentioned before, I've always wanted to travel. That's what I was working toward here in Las Vegas, saving up to go exploring."

"Perfect. The question now would be whether you're willing to travel with *me*."

His intensity was hard to ignore, not that she would. "Yes. In fact, I am willing to do quite a number of things with you."

The intensity changed only slightly to include a lusty half-smile. "Excellent. Perhaps we should make up now."

"Haven't we already done that?"

His gaze moved from her face to the rumpled sheets on the bed and back again. His smile widened. "Yes. However, in order to make it official, I believe sex is required to seal the deal."

"Make up sex." A statement, not a question. She knew what he meant.

"Yes."

"Okay." They both stood up and his head nearly crashed into the ceiling. She lunged at him, and he swept her into his arms. He lowered his head for a crushing kiss that overwhelmed her as he always delivered.

Lina gave herself over to his expert care, relishing the fact that not only was her new husband an amazing lover, he also shared a fundamental core life desire to travel. They were perfect for each other.

They kissed and kissed and kissed and tore their clothing off and fell on to the bed for what she considered the ultimate make up sex.

Dalton was tender and demanding, methodical and exhilarating, and he had her screaming his name in no time, following with a growl of his own in sensual completion. Lina came down off the high of orgasm slowly.

Tempting fate had never been more satisfying than with a man she'd fallen in love with who happened to also be her husband and didn't have any other women in his life. Best make up sex ever.

They clung to each other, still not speaking after their blissful renewal.

Outside the trailer, the sound of a vehicle close by intruded on her idyllic private moment with Dalton. The window was open slightly to let in air as they made up officially.

The car's engine turned off, doors squeaked opened and then closed. The sound of footsteps in the gravel put her on alert. Someone was heading to their trailer, not next door. She stiffened in Dalton's arms. He lifted his head, listening. "Expecting company?" she asked in a whisper.

Before he responded or either of them could move, the booming sound of a shotgun round rocketed through the trailer at the same moment a ragged hole appeared in the door.

CHAPTER 16

Even though Dalton had been half expecting a forced entry, the blast of the shotgun startled him. The scent of gunpowder intruded and smoke coiled into the small space from the newly blasted hole in his trailer door.

He'd rolled away from Lina after mind-blowing make up sex, feeling more gratified than he'd ever been in his life, expecting to spend the next few hours snuggling in post sexually satisfied idleness.

Seconds later, he rallied his limited strength and threw his body on top of Lina's to protect her from whatever was about to come through the smoking doorway of his formerly secret safe house-turned-busy hub.

It was not lost upon him that this was an epically bad time to be caught. They were naked, vulnerable and weakened from amazing sexual satisfaction. Well, perhaps that was only his problem.

The issue was how monumentally he'd miscalculated the significance of the phone call to her friend and, even worse, the speed with which someone had been dispatched to check it out.

He hadn't thought anyone would find them so

quickly after the phone call Lina had made to her friend. That had been a grave mistake on his part and also puzzled him.

Lake Havasu was several hours from Ironwood. Even someone leaving before the call ended wouldn't be here yet without a supersonic jet. Had someone flown here? Did they have someone who owed the Dragovics a favor in every city and town?

Dalton rose off of Lina, motioning her to stay quiet and covered up by the sheet. He slid backward off the bed, turned and grabbed his jeans off the floor as someone entered his trailer uninvited. Scooping up Lina's things, he tossed them onto the bed. She immediately started getting dressed beneath the sheet.

The still-smoking remains of his front door crashed against the outside of his trailer as someone yanked it open. He saw a gun in the open space followed quickly by a head.

"Get out!" Dalton put his pants on as quickly as possible and carefully zipped his fly as a familiar-looking dark-haired man with a smirk disregarded his command and stepped inside.

Unfortunately, Dalton's weapon was in the glove box at the front of the fifth wheel. There was another gun hidden beneath the driver's seat, neither of which he could access now. He made a mental note to put a firearm in the small bedroom area one of these days.

"What do you want?" Dalton asked, although he knew exactly what the guy wanted.

"Her," he said, confirming Dalton's guess. "She comes with us."

"Over my dead body."

"If you insist," he said, but didn't make a move with his weapon.

From behind him, Lina screamed, "No!" The guy still didn't move.

After a few seconds, a smirk formed. He said in an accented voice, "The widow shacking up with bounty hunter sent to bring her back is cliché, yes? Given your reputation, I'm surprised."

"Like I said before: Get out of my house."

"I will depart as soon as I retrieve widow." He tilted his head to one side and called out, "Nikolina, come along. It's past time to do your duty."

From behind Dalton, Lina said loudly, "I'm not leaving. If you make me, you'd better guard your privates."

The man frowned, but quickly recovered his composure. "You will come, Nikolina. Now."

"No. She stays with me." Dalton moved forward a step, keeping his body planted in the center of his domain to keep the stranger's wandering eyes from Lina.

The man smiled widely, but it was an evil smile of superiority. "Not an option, I'm afraid. If you wanted to hide widow, you shouldn't have used your name on car rental agreement, Mr. Dalton Langston." He made a tsking noise.

"Speaking of names, you have me at a disadvantage. What name do you go by?" Dalton asked.

The stranger seemed taken aback by the question. "You may call me Kirill."

Dalton folded his arms over his chest. "Hmm. Is that a first or a last name?"

"It's only name. What difference does it make?"

He shrugged. "No skin off my ass, just want to bill the correct person for the damage to my property." He gestured to the gaping hole in the door. "Who do you work for, Kirill? Did you want the bill to go to you or your employer?"

Dalton heard Lina behind him. He half turned to wave her back to bed, but she'd already put her feet on the floor and was shoving a sock-covered foot into one shoe.

"I work for parents," Kirill stated clearly. "She has duty back in Ironwood. I have papers to ensure cooperation."

Ah. The warrant. Dalton mentally heaved a sigh. Perhaps he should have lied to the Dragovics about taking their case. Lina's father must have hired Kirill as a backup.

Kirill was definitely the smartly dressed guy he'd seen at the bus station. He'd also be willing to bet he was the man Lina had kneed in the jewels in front of her apartment building. Perhaps he hadn't come from Ironwood, but Las Vegas. How did he have the ability to gain access to the rental car information? Given that the Dragovics were involved, it was entirely possible illegal means had been used to acquire the information.

Dalton also wondered how this man had found Lina at her place. Hadn't Lina said the guy pretended to be Dalton? What sort of resources did Kirill have? Or perhaps the better question had to do with the Dragovics' substantial means, which were vast and obviously far reaching. A more sinister thought occurred to him. Was Kirill following Dalton? Was that how he'd discovered Lina's whereabouts so quickly?

Kirill took another step forward. "Stand aside."

"No."

"I don't want to hurt you, Langston, but I will to bring widow back. Let her go. The parents will compensate you for her time in your care. I will even speak positively on your behalf."

"That's funny." Dalton smiled at him with his best superior look. "You'd better start reconsidering your goals."

"It's not my nature to change, ever. Don't be greedy, Langston. Give widow to me now or face consequences." Kirill took another small step forward, but his expression seemed a shade unsure.

Dalton didn't know what the fuck the guy meant about being greedy, unless her parents had put out a reward for her instead of a warrant for her detainment. Either way, he wasn't handing her over without a fight.

"Give widow to me."

"She's not a widow any longer."

Kirill stopped moving. A puzzled look registered on his face. "What is your meaning?"

"Nikolina is my wife. We got married in Las Vegas before leaving town. Tell her parents she's no longer their concern. She's mine now."

"That was a foolish mistake, my friend."

"You aren't my friend."

Kirill ducked his head in a surprising show of agreement at first before shifting to another more skeptical filled expression.

Dalton's focus was on the incredulous look his opponent suddenly exhibited, and not the weapon that appeared in the open door frame and centered on his chest.

The last thing he heard was the loud sound of the shot. The last thing he felt was a burning pain exploding in his chest, head and limbs all at once. His body fell into darkness as his legs gave way to the unyielding pull of gravity.

Lina screamed the moment she heard the shot. Dalton fell to his knees as if suddenly boneless. Once down, he shuddered a moment and then slumped to the floor in a heap, not moving.

She launched herself off the bed, landing at Dalton's side. Before she could see where he'd been shot, Kirill grabbed her arm, hauled her to her feet and dragged her over Dalton's body.

"Let's go, Nikolina. You have a lot of explaining to do with this endless fiasco."

"He's not breathing," she said, trying to wrench herself free and help Dalton. Kirill slapped her face hard enough for her to see stars when she tried to reach for him.

Her wits briefly scrambled, Kirill easily manhandled her out of the trailer. Two other thugs were waiting outside. Halfway to the vehicle, Lina started struggling like her life depended on it. They might take her, but she wasn't going without a fight.

She opened her mouth, shrieking into the air, hoping a bystander would intervene. Kirill, following close behind, slapped his hand over her mouth to silence her.

"If someone comes for rescue, their death goes on your conscience, Nikolina," he whispered. She stopped making noise and closed her eyes, sending out a plea that Dalton was not dead. The mere thought sent melancholy through her instantly.

Still, she struggled, not intending to make this abduction easy. It took three tries for them to get all of her limbs away from the frame and through the open back car door.

They shoved her headfirst into the backseat of their vehicle. She screamed in frustration at being thwarted. Kirill followed her into the rear of the car and promptly pushed a gun into her ribcage, and growled a sinister command. "Do not test me."

The vehicle jerked into motion and pulled away from the trailer.

"I can't kick you between the legs right now, but the first opportunity I get, you'd better protect yourself."

Kirill's expression darkened, but he remained silent. The gun barrel didn't move.

"Cooperate or I will make you do so."

She smirked. "You can't make me cooperate. I will never—"

Before she finished her empty threat, Kirill pulled a syringe from seemingly out of nowhere and jammed it into her shoulder through her shirtsleeve. She felt it when the content was injected.

"What was that?"

Kirill's only response was to remove the syringe and hand it to one of the thugs in the front seat.

Lina asked several more questions, but Kirill only stared at her with an amused expression. She turned away from him, putting her focus out the window. She could barely see anything, the tint was so dark, and eventually the sway of the vehicle and whatever Kirill had drugged her with pulled her into a troubled slumber. She hated sleeping, but traveling in a moving vehicle had always made her lethargic and drowsy. Whatever drug she'd been given only made her go to sleep faster.

She didn't wake until the vehicle slowed to a stop and the engine turned off. She sat up disoriented, unsure where she was, discovering a monstrous headache forming. Whatever drug he'd given her had been powerful.

The memory of Dalton slumped on the floor sent her emotions spiraling into despair. Her eyes welled up with tears, which didn't help the growing pain in her head. Her door was snatched open. Kirill grabbed her by the arm and yanked her out of the car and onto the concrete floor of what looked and smelled like an abandoned and musty warehouse.

"Where am I?" Her voice sounded asleep.

"Someplace where your bounty hunter friend will never find you," Kirill said.

"Does that mean he's alive?"

"Of course. I don't kill allies."

Lina didn't know what confounded her more, the idea that Dalton was somehow in league with this dangerous man or that he might be dead if not an ally. Both notions were deplorable to consider.

"He's not your ally," she said defiantly, hoping Dalton was alive and on her side. He had to be. He'd married her to keep her safe.

Kirill laughed. "Isn't he? You are here with me now waiting for my employers to come and explain what they want from you."

"So what, you shot him? You don't even know if he's still alive." *Please be alive. Please be alive.*

"Is it true what Langston said?"

"What?"

"About getting married before leaving Las Vegas. Is that true?"

Lina smiled in triumph. "Yes. It's true. We are married. The marriage is legal and has already been consummated, repeatedly." She felt her face heat up, but didn't care if Kirill saw her blush. He could suck it.

Kirill retrieved his phone and started typing furiously on it. After several minutes, he pushed out a long sigh. "I had hoped bounty hunter lied about marriage to protect you from retrieval."

Lina smirked, feeling superior. Her parents couldn't force her to marry anyone else. No one could force her to do anything. She wouldn't sign annulment papers. Nor would she sign divorce papers.

She and Dalton loved each other. They were going to travel together and see the world, making mad and passionate love each time they stopped in a new city.

"That is unfortunate."

"Why?"

"Dissolution of marriage, even for a quick Las Vegas wedding, takes time. Parents will not be happy."

"I don't care if my parents are happy. You can tell them I said so. I will never marry the other Zupan son. Never. Let me go. No harm, no foul."

Kirill shook his head. "I don't know your parents, but I suspect they won't be too happy about this wedding to the bounty hunter, either, for different reasons."

"What are you talking about? Didn't my parents hire you to bring me back to do my duty?"

From behind her came a new voice, a more heavily accented one that she'd never heard before. "No. I hired Kirill to find you and bring you to me." The man moved into view. He was an average-sized man, very thin with dark hair, a graying goatee and wire-framed glasses. She guessed he was of an age with her father, or older.

Kirill moved in front of Lina, surprising her. "Wait. There has been a development that is unexpected."

"What development? Never mind. I don't care. I want to sign the papers right now. Everything else can wait."

"I refuse to sign any papers," Lina said, but no one seemed to be listening to her.

Kirill shook his head at the other man. "Unfortunately, paper signing is not possible today."

"Why not?"

"Nikolina married the bounty hunter Dragovic sent after her in Las Vegas. I checked a few minutes ago. Papers are filed already. Sorry, but union between them is official."

The thin man didn't say anything for the space of five seconds. He stared at Kirill. He then turned his focus on her. Hands fisted until his knuckles turned white, the man lifted both arms up, keeping his elbows at his sides as if he were about to step into a boxing ring for a bout.

His breathing sped, his face turned a dark shade of crimson. His whole body started shaking, just a tremble at first then increasing until he looked like he was having a self-induced seizure.

He tilted his head back, opened his mouth and

screamed, "Fuck!" to the rafters of the warehouse for a solid ten seconds.

The man's color went blotchy. It couldn't be healthy. After a few more minutes, he seemed to calm himself down. Lina was terrified.

"Where is the bounty hunter?"

Kirill shrugged. "Back in Lake Havasu slumped in heap."

"Dead?"

"No."

"Why didn't you bring him here?"

Kirill pointed a thumb over his shoulder at Lina. "You paid me to find widow and bring her. So I find widow and bring her."

The thin man started pacing. "If the bounty hunter was dead, she'd be a widow again."

"Woman with two dead husbands days after each marriage brings other problems and links those difficulties to your name. Is unwise." Kirill studied the other man, seemingly unfazed by his overt anger.

"Are you certain the marriage in Las Vegas is even binding?"

Kirill nodded. "Marriage is valid. My suggestion after meeting him is you buy him off and hope he isn't indebted to Dragovic family."

"Yes. Thank you, Kirill, for sharing the obvious," the thin man said sarcastically. "You should have brought the bounty hunter here anyway."

Kirill shrugged. "If I had brought him, you would have been angry he saw you and could identify you."

"He doesn't know me."

"How do you know what he knows? He found Nikolina in one day after everyone looked for months. Perhaps he has other skills. You do not need to be identified by anyone else. You being here is not legal. If anyone sees you, it causes many other problems.

"Also, you don't know what arrangement bounty hunter made with Dragovics. Perhaps he intended to split money with them all along. Perhaps they only pretend to look for her."

"What money?" Lina asked. She hadn't meant to speak, but following their conversation had been very interesting. As was often true in her family during previous discussions of money and financial plans, no one tempered their chats in front of her, a mere girl.

Her parents had done so only at her expense, knowing she would never agree to the new stipulations set forth by the Zupan family regarding a second marriage to their other son. Realization struck.

"You are Pavel Zupan," she said, wondering why her first husband's father would pay to find her. What papers did he want her to sign? What money was involved?

Perhaps she should make a deal with Mislav's father instead of hoping her parents would do the right thing by her.

Kirill shook his head and gave her a look that said she should keep her mouth shut. "Do not speak."

"How do you know who I am?" the older man said with quiet rage in his tone.

"I figured it out. No one else besides my father would care about anyone I'm married to. You wanted me to marry your other son. You defaulted on the original agreement with my parents and demanded children in the second deal before you'd give them what they already considered theirs financially.

"My parents agreed to a second arranged marriage without consulting me. In fact, they tried to trick me into it because they knew I'd never agree to the new terms, so I left to live my own life. As far as I'm concerned, nothing has changed except my current marital status. I will not marry your other son, Mr. Zupan. And I don't believe you can make me."

"I believe I could." An oily smile appeared on his smug face.

"I'm already married to Dalton. Plus, I seem to recall hearing that you aren't allowed to travel within this country, Mr. Zupan. I suspect you aren't here legally."

The color in his cheeks flamed up again.

"What do you want to do with her?" Kirill said.

Zupan stared at her for an uncomfortably long time. He seemed to come to some decision, if the expression on his face was accurate. He pulled his phone out, put it to his ear and started talking to someone as he walked away. It was unclear if he'd made a call or if someone had called him.

When Zupan returned, his air of triumph was even stronger.

"Let's go."

"Where are you taking me?" Lina asked.

"Let's let it be a surprise, shall we?"

CHAPTER 17

Dalton spent at least fifteen minutes incapacitated before waking up in a heap on the floor of his safe house trailer after being shot with the Taser. Once he could move again, he called his brother, Deke.

"Quick question."

"Okay, shoot," Deke said.

"Yes or no—do you have any contacts in Lake Havasu with a private jet that could get me to Ironwood immediately?"

There was silence on the line for maybe a count of three. "Maybe," his twin brother said warily.

"That's not a yes or a no."

Deke sighed deeply. "Let me make a quick phone call."

"I eagerly wait to hear from you."

In less than five minutes, Deke called back. "You do have quite the lucky streak going, Dalton, I'll give you that much."

Dalton sighed in relief. "Tell me."

"Head to the regional airport, go to hanger seven, talk to a guy named Bosworth. He has a trip planned to Ironwood leaving in twenty minutes. He promised to add you to the passenger roster and even wait for you as a favor to me."

"Thanks, Deke. I owe you."

"No worries. I'll expect a good story at the next Key West gathering."

"Done." Dalton hung up. He grabbed a few things, including Lina's two bags, and headed for the airport. Less than two hours after calling Deke, the plane set down in Ironwood. During his flight, he'd contemplated several scenarios and sent messages seeking information from various sources the moment they touched down. In the short term, and with any luck, he'd beat Kirill to town and already be waiting at Lina's parents' home for her to show up or at least arrive closely after they did.

He grabbed a taxi to his apartment, stowed Lina's things in his bedroom closet and took his own vehicle to visit the Dragovic household. Located on the edge of town behind a security force that rivaled that of most government buildings, the Dragovic family lived on a well-appointed fifty-acre property.

Dalton pulled up to the guard shack in front of an iron gate that protected the driveway leading to the house. He wasn't certain what reception he'd get, but if they didn't let him in through the gates, he'd find another way inside.

The guard called the main house to announce him, nodding and practically coming to attention as he listened to someone on the other end of the line, then he quickly opened the gates and gestured Dalton through before hanging up the phone.

Dalton didn't need to be told twice. He waved at the guard and sped through when the iron gates opened enough to allow his vehicle through. Once he got to the circular driveway, he parked at the front door, took the flagstone stairs two at a time and pounded his fist on an ornately carved set of wooden doors that had to be twelve feet tall.

A servant opened the door, allowing him entrance

without any grief. Once inside the marble dominated entryway, the servant didn't seem to be in as much of a hurry to lead him to Dragovic.

Dalton had to tamp down the urge to race through the house screaming for Lina's father. Maybe he should have been screaming Lina's name, but he didn't think she'd made it here yet.

After what felt like an hour of slow travel, Dalton was led into what looked like the library.

"Langston," Ivan Dragovic called from across the room. "Are you alone? I expected that you'd already found Lina and had brought her home."

"I did find Lina," Dalton said. "Then someone shot his way into my place and kidnapped her. Why would anyone do that? What do you know, Dragovic? Tell me now."

Dragovic frowned. "Kidnapped!"

"Yes. Can we forgo the shock and great acting skills? I know it was you. Kirill said he worked for the parents. Tell me where she is. What did you do with her?"

"Kirill?" Dragovic said the name with the same reaction as someone walking over his grave. Eyes wide at first, then quickly shuttered, Dragovic exhaled a short breath as if shocked to his soul. Dalton wouldn't have been surprised to see him gesture a sign of the cross over his chest.

"Who is he to you?" Dalton asked.

Dragovic walked closer. "I know someone named Kirill who works for Pavel Zupan, my daughter's father-in-law."

Dalton wanted to ensure Dragovic was enlightened as to his and Lina's new relationship. "There is something you need to know."

Dragovic smiled indulgently. "I'm certain there are an abundance of things I need to know. Right now I want to know who has my daughter, if it's Pavel

Zupan, and why you changed your mind about our arrangement?"

"I didn't change my mind about our arrangement. However, Pavel Zupan is no longer Lina's father-in-law."

"What are you talking about?"

"I married Nikolina in Las Vegas two days ago."

When his face morphed into an expression the very definition of shock, it was clear that Lina's father had no forewarning or prior knowledge of their marriage. Kirill had been talking about the parents of her first husband. Dalton had been plagued by the feeling that heading to the Dragovic compound had been too easy, that he was on the wrong track, although it had been his singular choice until now. Knowing who Kirill worked for would have been handy information earlier.

"You did what?! You married *my* Nikolina?" Dragovic raged.

"Yes."

Dragovic's face went nearly purple with wrath. He started pacing. "What would possess you to do such a thing?"

"I love her."

He stopped pacing. "No. I don't believe it." His gaze narrowed. "You married her because my daughter didn't want to do her duty and wed the Zupan heir."

Dalton lifted one shoulder in shrug, not able to completely discount any or all of Lina's reasons for marrying him. It may have been a factor, but it didn't matter. He intended to keep her.

"Be that as it may, I love her."

"I'll have it annulled."

Dalton shook his head. "Too late for that, I'm afraid."

"You slept with my daughter!" Dragovic grated out angrily between clenched teeth. His sudden riveting stare was fierce and unyielding.

The look Dalton returned was equally ferocious. "I slept with my wife, yes."

Dragovic suddenly went very calm, which bothered Dalton more than his edge-of-violence reaction. The man inhaled deeply and exhaled noisily, calming his demeanor significantly. After a quiet minute, Dragovic said, "A divorce——"

"Is out of the question," Dalton finished for him. "As I've said repeatedly, I love her. I'm keeping her as my wife. What I want to hear from you is where Kirill and Mr. Zupan would take her."

"How would I know where they'd take her? Pavel Zupan isn't even allowed in this country. Likely Kirill is operating under his direction from afar."

"Okay, better yet, call him and demand information. Find out where Kirill would take her." Dalton didn't have time to take another wrong turn. He needed to know where his wife was.

An interesting expression came over Dragovic's face, as though a new thought had just occurred to him. "I won't call him."

"Then give me the number and I'll call."

"No."

"Why not?"

"I do not answer to you. Your impudent marriage to my daughter may have cost me a large financial dividend."

"She's not the prize cow at a fair that you can buy and sell. She is a human being. She is your daughter. But right now she is also my wife and you'd better get used to that fact."

Dragovic frowned, but before he said anything, an elegant woman swept into the room. "Is this the bounty hunter, Ivan?" Without waiting for a response, she turned to Dalton. "Did you find my daughter? Where is she?"

"He found her and then he married her," Dragovic

said, the accusation in his tone filling the large room.

Lina's mother stopped moving and stared at her husband. "He did what?" She looked back at Dalton, an unattractive sneer forming on her lips as her gaze swept him from head to feet and back again. A frown settled on her face at the idea of her precious daughter marrying someone like him.

"He married her and slept with her."

Lina's mother crossed her arms and pushed out a very long sigh of disappointment. "How long will a divorce take?"

"I'm not divorcing her," Dalton said.

"You will do what we tell you."

Laughter rumbled from his chest before he could stop it. "No. I won't." Dalton experienced an epiphany in that moment. Poor Lina. No wonder she'd run. He shouldn't have come here. Now he'd have to search for Kirill using different criteria. Dalton scanned the room, looking for the best way to leave without having to cross in front of either of Lina's parents.

Before he could search out an escape route, the phone on the desk rang loud and long. Dragovic crossed the room to bark into the handset, "What?"

If Dalton thought Ivan Dragovic had been angry before, he was mistaken. The man frowned as color filled his face once more, and shook with fury as someone spoke to him on the phone.

"Where?" he asked, grating out the word like each letter pained him. Dragovic looked up and zeroed his gaze on Dalton. Was this call about Lina? He took a step in Dragovic's direction, intent on wrestling the phone from him. He wanted to reach through the line and strangle Kirill.

"Is that Kirill?" Dalton asked, moving toward Dragovic.

"Yes, but I need more time to make that

arrangement," Dragovic said into the phone. He listened, his gaze darting from Dalton to his wife several times as Dalton stalked him.

"Fine. I'll ensure his presence." He hung up the phone and straightened his frame, staring at Dalton as he made it to the front edge of the massive desk. "That was Kirill."

"What does he want? Or rather, where is he? I want to go retrieve my wife."

"He has invited all of us to meet in an hour."

"Is that so?" Dalton wasn't fooled. Whatever this was, it was absolutely not in his favor or Lina's.

"Kirill, directed by Mr. Zupan of course, wants to meet and discuss terms."

"Terms? No. There are no terms I'm interested in talking about beyond retrieving my wife."

Dragovic frowned. "If you don't agree to an immediate dissolution of marriage to my daughter, I'm not certain what will be in store for you."

"Well, I do know what will be in store." Dalton was fairly certain Kirill and Mr. Zupan had no compunction about killing him and making her a widow again. "I will ensure my wife is safe." He stopped short of stating the rest of his intentions. He would grab her up and run until they were both safe.

Although, a woman with two dead husbands in a short time span often had a stench of its own in any cultural circle regarding future marriages, it was especially true in the old county beliefs of Kzeratia.

If they wanted him dead so Lina could marry the other Zupan son, he was in for a fight unlike any other, but he hoped superstition would be in his favor in this matter.

"Persuasion will be used to entice you. I believe they wish to offer you money to sign divorce papers. I will match whatever they offer."

Dalton didn't say what he wanted to, which was, "Fuck no!" There wasn't a sum they could name that would entice him to leave Lina. But they didn't know that. Perhaps it would be best to pretend he did have a number. "I don't think you can count that high."

Dragovic laughed. A rumble started low in his chest until he shook with mirth. "Then you don't know me very well."

"True. So here is what I will do. I'll go with you. I'll listen to the 'offer' and consider your silent match amount before making my final decision."

Lina's father nodded, looking satisfied, as if he'd already won this battle with a mere payoff. He probably believed that everyone had a price. But he didn't know Dalton.

Dragovic called for a car to be brought around for them, and then had an intense conversation with Lina's mother, who insisted on coming to the meeting.

In the end, Dragovic relented, making Dalton feel better. If his wife came along, perhaps the violence could be kept to a minimum. While Dalton hated the notion of Dragovic thinking he'd won this round using greed, it was only for the short term.

For now, if Dalton couldn't see Lina, he couldn't ensure she was safe. He'd promised to protect her and he intended to do it regardless of the half-truths he spouted to her father.

Once they were together again, he'd move heaven and earth to spirit her away from any and all parents with an agenda that didn't match their own. The only downfall he anticipated was that if he was successful, he'd likely have to put them both into a witness protection program to keep Lina safe. But that was a worry for another time.

First get Lina into his immediate presence and then ensure she knew he'd never leave her or divorce her.

Then he'd do his damnedest to stay alive and keep the promises he'd made to her regarding traveling to his favorite places to show her interesting sights.

If he had to change both of their names this time to ensure complete safety, so be it.

The worst thought ever suddenly came into his head. If he put them both into witness protection, she'd be safe from her family, but he'd also have to give up *his* family in the bargain. Never seeing his brothers or parents again made a sick knot form in his belly, but he took pains to cover it.

Dragovic watched him, looking as satisfied as if he'd already won. Dalton wanted to knock him down a few pegs, but waited for a better opportunity to do so. He was desperate to get Lina in his sights. Being without her and unsure of her circumstances was more disheartening than he could ever have imagined and even worse than the idea of leaving his family forever.

Dalton shook off his despair and silently plotted. He used his skills to get into the minds of the men he was about to face. Who were they? What did they want? How could he keep them from winning? All the while, Lina's sweet face with that half smile of rebellion remained at the forefront of his thoughts.

He unobtrusively started checking things out on his phone. If he could discover what motivated them beyond money, he'd be closer to figuring out how to play the coming negotiations.

Dalton would do his utmost to keep her, knowing in his soul that if it came down to it, he'd let her go so she could live even if it wasn't with him rather than risk her life to remain married. It was a horrible thought he hated to contemplate as he searched his phone for any and all helpful information, seeing little in the way of anything useful thus far.

CHAPTER 18

Lina overheard the phone call to her father and the deal that had been set in motion. The good news was their first option wasn't to kill Dalton outright. The bad news was they were hell-bent on dissolving their marriage so Lina could be forced to marry Marko Zupan.

Pavel Zupan was singular in his intent to see his remaining son married to her. Lina just didn't understand why it seemed so vital to accomplish this sooner rather than later.

She'd understood the Zupan family wanting to wait for the full mourning year, at least until she'd run away during negotiations. That had been a large part of her impetus to leave and hide out in the first place. She hadn't wanted a year's worth of time for them to come up with an ironclad way to get her to sign her life away.

Kirill had bound her with handcuffs and attached her to a table like a criminal in a television show at the police station about to be sent up the river. She wished a lawyer or a phone call was due her. In this situation, she suspected the longer she remained silent the better off she'd be.

If she thought being difficult would result in her freedom she would have been the worst hellion Kirill had ever faced. But on the way here, resistance had only gotten her drugged. She was still a bit muddle-headed. Besides, in listening to their plans, she got the impression they wanted Dalton to renounce her more than anything.

That they didn't want him dead outright was only due to superstitions regarding the demise of not one but two husbands in a short time. It was a frightening proposition attached to a female of marriageable age in their old-fashioned culture. Also this was the first time she'd ever been grateful for a steadfast adherence to tradition.

Lina remained silent, listening to everything they said.

After the call to her father, Pavel Zupan called his remaining son, Marko. It seemed the entire Zupan family had traveled to this country to straighten out the whole marriage mess left behind with the death of their first son.

Zupan's second call had also been rife with drama, surprisingly enough. Lina only heard Zupan's side of the conversation, but it sounded like Marko didn't want to marry her either. Perhaps that would help her.

Then again, perhaps he mourned his brother. It had been less than four months since Mislav had died. If they'd been close, perhaps he found the idea of marrying his brother's widow before the allotted year of mourning ended abhorrent. Or perhaps he found the idea of marrying her at all distasteful. Maybe she had a secret ally.

Once Marko showed up, she planned to ensure he knew about her current husband, Dalton, and that she was no longer untouched regarding the marriage bed. Marko needed to understand exactly what he was getting if he was a foe in this matter. Still, getting Marko on their side was her best idea as far as keeping Dalton as her husband and getting all the parents off their backs with regard to the future she wanted.

Lina longed to see Dalton. He'd been at her father's home as the one-sided conversation had progressed. It was a surprise, since she'd worried about his being alive at all. She'd wanted to shout and demand she be allowed to talk to her husband, but resisted the urge. The time was not right to be difficult. She wanted to ensure Dalton was actually alive before making any further plans. She didn't trust any of the assembled people or her father to utter any kind of truth unless she could see it with her own eyes.

Once reunited with Dalton, to see he was unharmed, she'd do her best to make life as difficult as she could for Kirill, Zupan and her parents. Perhaps Marko Zupan would be an ally, but if not, she added him to her list of who to be difficult to.

Lina only knew *she* would not be managed. *She* would not be dictated to. *She* had her own plans. Unless… A terrible thought came into her head.

Would she be willing to give Dalton up if it meant saving his life? Yes. Would she throw herself on a sword to save him, give up her life and dreams in order to marry Marko Zupan if it meant Dalton would live? Again, yes.

Zupan, like her parents, planned to sway Dalton with money. It was all they knew. All they thought was needed to get what they wanted. Lina didn't think Dalton was ruled by monetary gain. He'd been willing to give up the job to bring her to her parents and he'd married her to protect her, hadn't he?

Another difficult thought occurred. Dalton marrying her had also given him a certain amount of power. He'd have to agree to divorce her at this point to give everyone what they wanted. Lina's ultimate marital freedom to wed Marko Zupan was all the parents' singular goal.

Had she misread Dalton? Was there an amount of

money that he could be swayed by? A price he had in mind as a perfect payoff? She hoped not. At this point, the only thing she looked forward to was seeing Dalton alive with her own eyes.

Once they were together, though, negotiations would begin. Lina's only plan consisted of being difficult and refusing to divorce Dalton. She glanced at Kirill. He had a large gun tucked into the back of his pants.

All too soon, the sound of a vehicle outside the warehouse was heard. Several car doors opened and closed. Kirill went to open the large warehouse door to admit Dalton first, her father next and, surprisingly, her mother.

Dalton's gaze immediately searched the room. Once he saw her, he started moving quickly in her direction. Before he'd gotten within ten feet of her seat, he yelled, "Kirill, take the handcuffs off my wife this instant." He covered the space between them quickly, wrapping his arm around her shoulders. He kissed her and whispered, "Are you all right, Lina?"

She nodded, unwanted tears forming and spilling onto her face at the joy of being with him again. He put his large hand over her bound wrists, asking, "Did he hurt you? Tell me the truth."

She shook her head. "No. He just kept me from you. That was enough." Lina rattled her cuffs against the metal table.

"Kirill!" Dalton said loudly over one shoulder. "Release Lina this instant or you can shove any coming offer up your ass."

Kirill sauntered over with a smug expression. "See, I told you, Nikolina. He *will* take the money and divorce you."

"Dalton," she started to say, as Kirill released first one cuff and then the other. Once she was free, she wrapped her arms round her husband's neck. "I was afraid they'd killed you."

"Shh. I'm fine. I'm sorry I couldn't keep him from taking you."

"He shot you and left you unconscious on the floor of the trailer. I understand that you're psychic and everything about hunting people, but I don't see how either of us could have prevented our current circumstances."

Dalton pushed out a sigh. He pulled back and stared into her eyes. "I won't risk your life, Lina. I've thought about what may happen in the next few minutes, and bottom line, you being alive is the only thing that matters to me."

Kirill snorted from a few feet away. "That means he intends to take the very generous offer to divorce you, Nikolina."

"Fuck off, Kirill," he said loud enough for her parents and Zupan, who'd all approached, to hear.

Lina stood up carefully, keeping herself attached to Dalton. She looked in her parents' direction, hoping to see some of the same concern in their expressions as to her safety, but only found the usual disappointed look she typically got when she did something they disapproved of.

Her mother said impatiently, "Nikolina, come here."

"No. I belong with him. We're married. I want to stay with Dalton. Nothing will convince me to leave him or divorce him and annulment is out of the question. I may already carry his child."

Her father didn't look surprised. "I don't care about that."

Zupan took a step closer. "I'll give you five million dollars to sign the papers for annulment right now, Mr. Langston."

Lina sucked in a gasp. Five million dollars! Her father grunted in Zupan's direction, but said, "And I'll match that amount, as I promised before we came here, if you agree to sign the papers to dissolve your marriage to my daughter."

What the hell was going on? Dalton had just been offered ten million dollars to divorce her and walk away. *She* might even be briefly tempted, given such an offer. Desolation filled her. They were all very serious. They wanted her to marry Zupan's remaining son, and they were all willing to fork over quite a lot of money to ensure she did so.

She was doomed.

Lina looked up into Dalton's face, expecting to see that shiny look of greedy desire in his eyes. The same look her parents got after a particularly satisfying day when they'd added a large sum to their bank account.

Dalton, to his credit, didn't look like he cared a whit about the vast sum. He also didn't seem very surprised by their offer.

In fact, seconds later he smiled as if in disbelief and snorted as though they were lowballing him. "Oh, you'll have to do better than that, gentlemen. I thought you were motivated in this matter." He laughed and grabbed Lina's hand. "Let's go, lovely wife of mine. They obviously aren't serious about separating us."

He took two steps with her in tow before Zupan stopped him. "What figure did you have in mind, Mr. Langston?"

Dalton stopped, let go of her hand and wrapped his arm around her shoulders, pulling her tight to his side. "Let's start the bidding at nine figures and see if Mr. Dragovic will match *that* amount, shall we?"

"Nine figures!" Zupan growled. "Do you mean to say one hundred million dollars?"

Lina's father coughed and the purple hue showed up on his face, exactly like when he was angry about spending money. Any money. "You are insane. I will *never* match one hundred million dollars!"

Dalton shrugged and started them moving toward the warehouse exit.

"Wait!" Zupan called. "Fine. One hundred million dollars."

Her father sounded like he was choking. "I refuse to match that ludicrous amount. It's too much."

"Doesn't matter. I said you should *start* at nine figures. Make it five hundred million and I won't walk out of here right this instant," Dalton said as calmly as if he was talking about pocket change. "Each," he added.

Lina looked up into her husband's serene face and wondered if he'd lost his mind. His gaze caressed her. He smiled as if maybe he wouldn't let her go for any amount. Lina felt cherished, appreciated and most of all loved for the first time in her life. To be loved more than money was a rare ideal in her experience.

"I love you," she whispered.

Dalton took his wife in his arms, lifted her to her tippy toes and kissed her like he'd wanted to since entering the room. Her whispered, "I love you," made him more certain than ever that he didn't want to leave her. Ever. There was no amount of money they could offer that he'd accept in trade for her.

Lina's mother shouted, "Let her go, you Neanderthal! I will not let this stand. Nikolina, come over here this instant."

She broke away from him, turned to her mother and said, "No. I love him. He loves me. We love each other. Please just let us go. If you want Marko to run your business so desperately, then adopt him or simply put him in charge. You don't need me."

"Tradition be damned then?" her mother asked incredulously. "I'm ashamed of you for even voicing such ridiculous ideas. You will divorce this inappropriate man. You will marry the other Zupan boy and fulfill your obligation."

Lina straightened. "No. I fulfilled the dictates of the traditional first marriage. I have no further obligation."

"Nikolina!" her mother shouted, motioning her over again sharply.

Lina shook her head. "You swore to me I'd be free after the first marriage. If I'm still obligated, then you lied to me and that's worse. Honestly, I don't care if you are ashamed of me. You should be ashamed of yourselves. I have married someone I love. You should be happy for me. Let us go. Find another way to link our family to the Zupans. There must be some other way."

Kirill crossed his arms and said, "I wonder if your husband is as infatuated with you as he is with the money he'll get staying married to you, Nikolina."

"What are you talking about?" Lina asked. "I don't have any money."

At the same exact time, Zupan said, "Shut up, Kirill!" and sent a worried look toward Lina's parents.

On the flight to Ironwood, Dalton had done a quick search on his phone and sent a detailed message to Deke asking his twin to do some information gathering for him.

During the time he spent flying to Arizona in the very nice private jetliner accommodations Deke had arranged, his brother had found quite a bit of interesting information on the Zupan family, currently of Kzeratia. He'd sent what he learned at the perfect time, too, just as Dalton traveled to the warehouse for this final stand.

Deke had somehow learned that the eldest Zupan son had been given access to a very generous trust fund the moment he married Lina. It was reported that the new knowledge of this trust fund and the sudden influx of cash may have contributed to Mislav's rather sudden demise. He'd gone on a wild streak, spending money rather foolishly.

The secret trust fund was about to be revealed. Dalton was surprised Kirill knew about it.

Zupan looked like he wanted to throttle Kirill for mentioning the bounty Lina had gained on the death of her husband. The lawyer hadn't adequately protected the funds or he forgot to include a prenuptial agreement. Either way, Lina became the sole recipient of the trust the moment her first husband died.

Kirill shrugged. "Langston already knows about the money. That's why he's asking for so much. He must have found out about the trust fund." Kirill pulled the gun from the back of his pants and pointed it at the ground.

"What trust fund?" Dragovic wanted to know.

Kirill continued, "What did you find out, Langston? How did you learn of the trust fund?"

Dalton grinned. "I'm well informed and I have tremendous resources that you probably can't imagine. One of my brothers easily found out about Mislav and his very expensive untimely death. It was also quite obvious what contributed to his sudden demise after the marriage papers were signed. The wild spending spree he went on directly after leaving a certain lawyer's office newly married was rather foolish in retrospect."

"Explain to me what you are talking about," Dragovic said, but no one seemed to be listening.

"Well, I'm fairly certain that I found the true reason you want me to divorce Lina. And I'd be willing to bet you didn't inform the Dragovic family of it either. Otherwise they would move heaven and earth to get back in her good graces. Whether or not she is swayed isn't really the issue, now is it?"

Dragovic shot an evil look at Zupan, which was returned in kind. "Don't listen to him. We both know the reason a divorce is necessary is so that we can expedite the marriage of your daughter and my son, Marko. They need to get married as soon as possible. I'll even forgo the yearlong mourning period and speed up the payment."

"Something is not right," Dragovic said to his wife. He turned to Dalton. "What do you know?"

Dalton opened his mouth, but Kirill lifted his gun. "Mr. Zupan doesn't wish for this information to come out." He then lowered the weapon away from Dalton, turned and pointed it at Zupan.

"I guess you shouldn't have opened your mouth and spilled the beans then, Kirill," Dalton said smugly.

"What is the meaning of this, Kirill?" Zupan looked like he was about to suffer an apoplectic seizure.

Dalton laughed. "He's obviously discovered the secret that I already know. You have little power, sir. You've trusted the wrong people."

Another car pulled up outside the warehouse. All eyes went to the noise except Dalton's. He kept his focus on the other parties.

A young man with the same build as Zupan strolled into the warehouse at a quick clip. His eyes searched the room and then landed on his father. This must be the future bridegroom all parties wanted Lina to marry after throwing him over.

"Marko?" Zupan seemed surprised to see his son. "I thought you weren't coming tonight."

Marko Zupan was younger than Dalton expected. Or perhaps he just looked younger. Mislav had been five years older. Dalton and Marko were actually the same age.

"I need to talk to you, Father. There is something I need to tell you and it has gone unsaid long enough."

"It's good that you are here, son," Zupan said. "Once the papers have been signed to dissolve Nikolina's marriage to this…man," he managed to grate out. Dalton figured he'd wanted to say "bastard interloper," but no matter. He'd also figured out what Marko was about to reveal. Deke's previous search and report had revealed quite a lot of interesting extra information.

Dalton had simply directed his twin to ask the right questions and search in the right places using The Organization's vast resources to discover what he needed to know for this meeting. Deke hadn't let him down.

"It doesn't matter if you dissolve her current marriage. I cannot marry Nikolina, to eventually become a US citizen," Marko said, glancing at Dalton and Lina. "In fact, I wouldn't even if I could."

Everyone in the room hushed and stopped moving.

"What in the world are you talking about?" Zupan turned to his son. "We agreed that the *only* option was for you to marry Nikolina and blend our family with the Dragovic's. You must become a US citizen. It's the only way. You know what is at stake. You know why this needs to happen."

Marko shrugged. "I've tried to tell you many times why it won't work, but you don't ever listen to me or allow me to speak."

Zupan looked around the room at the assembled crowd. His expression seemed like this wasn't the time he wanted to suddenly break down and listen to his son's heartfelt declarations, but after a few moments he cleared his throat. "Fine. Tell me, Marko, why is it such a difficulty for you to marry Nikolina Dragovic Zupan so that we can reacquire the vast trust fund technically in her possession?"

"Because I'm already married."

CHAPTER 19

Lina didn't know what she'd been expecting Marko to say, but being married wasn't even in the top ten of possible scenarios. She was quick to take advantage of the information, though. "Excellent. I'm already married. Marko is already married. No divorce or annulment is necessary at this time. Dalton, I'd like to leave."

Kirill pointed his gun into the air and fired. The echo of the shot reverberated throughout the warehouse. "No one leaves," he said in a low, dangerous tone.

Dalton pulled her closer into his arms as if to shield her from further gunfire. He glanced over his shoulder toward the darkened area of the warehouse. Did her husband plan an escape into the darkness? She readied herself to race away.

"I don't care who is married or not." Kirill moved toward Zupan. "I had planned to do things differently, but in light of this new information, perhaps I'll just demand my due. I have another option for you to consider."

"What option? And what do you think is due to you, Kirill?" Zupan asked with a frown.

Kirill marched closer to Zupan. "Do you not know who I am, old man?"

"You're someone who is about to be fired from my employ."

"Do I not look familiar to you? I am told I bear a striking resemblance to my mother."

Zupan stared deeply into Kirill's eyes as if a hint of recognition might be there, but he shook his head in denial. "I don't know who you are beyond the man I hired to do a job."

"No? Well, you are foolish and short-sighted. I am your firstborn, your bastard firstborn son. I am child you discarded to participate in arranged marriage for your family. Mislav, the son you claimed as your firstborn was an idiot, only worried about his own pleasures and vices, which killed him.

"Originally, I'd planned to kill Marko as well, but I discovered his secret and I knew he was no threat to me.

"Langston married Nikolina before I could do the same thing in Las Vegas. Although, I had a much more private ceremony in mind, one which would have held up in court, but Lina wasn't interested in even listening to me.

"Still, I planned to offer myself up to marry Nikolina, since I knew Marko was already spoken for. I figured I was your last hope, old man. I figured you would acknowledge me as your firstborn and promptly arrange a marriage with Nikolina as *my* wife."

"Why wouldn't I simply annul Marko's marriage?"

"Because I have a son," Marko said.

"What!" Zupan seemed stunned.

"My son was born two months ago. I've been married for over a year. So whatever plans you hatch today with Nikolina," Marko sent a brief, tired look her way, "the Dragovics and your bastard son, it has nothing to do with me. Not anymore. Or perhaps more accurately, it never did."

Zupan shook his head as if trying to clear away a fog. Marko turned and walked out of the warehouse. As both Kirill and Marko's revelations had been revealed, Dalton had been slowly and unobtrusively moving them half-step by half-step toward the unlit part of the warehouse. They'd managed to get quite a ways as surprising revelations flew around the room.

Standing behind her, one of Dalton's arms was wrapped securely around her waist, the other loosely dangled at his side. He had a plan and Lina did her best to sway silently toward the darkness, putting her full faith and trust in the man she loved beyond reason.

Dalton didn't say anything to her. They'd covered several feet of floor space before Kirill noticed.

"Where do you think you're going?"

Dalton yelled over her head and across the room, "I'm going out the back way!"

A loud thump echoed across the vast room and the warehouse plunged into immediate and complete obsidian darkness.

Dalton tightened his grip on her, dragging her backward to their original spot. There he pulled her to the ground as a shot rang out in the darkness.

"I will kill you, Langston!" Kirill screamed, his voice coming from seemingly nowhere and everywhere in the opaque color of the room.

From outside the warehouse several police car sirens pealed, swelling up and crashing into the darkness. Lina heard scuffling, but couldn't tell where the noise was coming from or where it was moving to.

She was on her side and Dalton was snuggled up behind her. The cold of the concrete floor seeped into her body, making her shiver. Her husband wrapped his arms more securely around her, pulling her into his body for warmth.

A disembodied voice speaking through a bullhorn

outside the warehouse said, "We have the place surrounded! Come out with your hands up!"

In her ear, Dalton chuckled. "Talk about cliché," he whispered. "Don't worry. I know that voice. It means we're saved."

In the darkness, Lina turned over, found Dalton's face by feeling for it, and placed her mouth on his. "I love you, Dalton," she whispered.

"I love you, too." As expected, her husband devoured her with his kiss, taking her away from the noise of the bullhorn, the darkness of their surrounds and the fear of reprisals from the Zupan family, Kirill, the murderous bastard henchman, or even her own parents in the moment.

A short time later, the lights came on, bright and intruding, but Dalton didn't stop kissing her. In fact, he stepped up the intensity of the lip-lock. She responded in kind, her mouth fairly scorched in the process.

Loud shouts and what sounded like a swarm of law enforcement people entered the place, barking orders for the others in the warehouse to surrender weapons and give up.

More noises could be heard from across the room, but she and Dalton were partly hidden behind a single crate stacked on top of a wooden pallet well away from the melee, as if in their own little cocoon.

Once things quieted and the others were marched outside, protesting all the way, a man's voice called out, "Dalton."

Dalton finally broke the kiss, and shouted, "Over here." He helped her to her feet as Lina wiped her swollen lips with the back of one hand.

The man who approached looked familiar. "You're Deke, right?" she asked when he was an arm's length away.

"That's right." Deke's gaze swept her briefly before

he turned toward Dalton and then back. "You must be Nikolina Dragovic."

"You can call me Lina," she said and then heat seared her cheeks. "Actually, I'm Lina Langston now. Thanks for the rescue."

"Wow. First of all, welcome to the family. And second of all, not that I don't appreciate your praise, but you should thank Dalton. Perhaps that's what you were just doing behind the crate. Thanking your husband." Deke grinned. "Regardless, Dalton is the one who set this all up. I'm merely an instrument of his diabolical master plan."

"Thanks, bro."

"No problem."

Lina said, "So tell me about Veronica."

Deke's brows furrowed. "You mean Alex's wife?"

She laughed. "Yes. That's exactly what I wanted to hear. That she's Alex's wife and not Dalton's former fiancée."

Dalton squeezed his arm around her shoulder. "Don't trust me, wife?"

"I trust you. I was just checking an alternate source for confirmation. No harm done, right?"

"I suppose not."

Deke snapped his fingers. "I get it. Mom sent you that picture of you and Veronica together, too."

"Yep."

Deke leaned in like he was about to tell her confidential information. "Veronica felt sorry for him. No one else did. But I can't wait until the next Key West trip. This will make an awesome story."

"What story?"

"Dalton went on vacation and ended up eloping in Las Vegas. I want to hear the story and repeat it in Key West."

"I'll tell my own story, thank you—" Before Dalton

said anything else, another man entered the warehouse.

"Deke. Dalton," he called out. "We have unfinished business."

"What's up, Miles?" Deke asked as the newcomer joined their small family circle. Lina had started to relax in light of Dalton and Deke's light brotherly banter. Now she began to tense up again.

"I thought you were on a journey from Ironwood to Las Vegas, Miles," Dalton said.

Miles shook his head. "I found someone else to take care of that job. Delegation is at the top of my skill set."

Without missing a beat, Miles rounded on her, asking, "Are you Nikolina Dragovic Zupan?"

She shrugged. "I guess." A smile shaped her lips. She was now Nikolina Dragovic Zupan Langston, to be completely accurate.

Miles pulled a set of handcuffs from the back of his belt and said, "Nikolina Zupan, I have a warrant for your arrest."

Chapter 20

"**Y**ou have the right to remain silent. Anything you say can and will be used against you in a court of law." Miles quickly finished advising Lina of her rights.

He grabbed her by the elbow, twirled her around and snapped one handcuff on her before Dalton was able to react and slap the other cuff out of his hand.

"What the fuck, Miles?"

"I'm sorry. But the only reason we were able to act on this whole diabolical plan of yours was with *this* warrant to arrest Nikolina Dragovic Zupan in conjunction with a stolen jewelry complaint."

"I didn't steal any jewelry." Nikolina pulled on the cuff, even though he'd left it very loose on her wrist.

Miles said, "I have no doubt about that. However, I must take you in and process you before anything further can happen. It's either me doing this or any one of several lettered agencies waiting outside anxious to do it. However, I prefer to be in charge, as I don't trust anyone else, as a rule."

Dalton straightened to his full height. "I'm coming with her."

"No. You will follow us there." Miles gave him a

look that said, "Please, trust me." Dalton wanted to, but watching Lina being packed off to jail rankled him.

"Where are you going to take her? The police station in Ironwood?" Dalton didn't think that was a good idea.

Miles glanced over one shoulder as if to ensure they were alone and then grinned. In a low tone he said, "No. Why would I go there? I'm headed directly for The Organization headquarters."

Deke put one hand on Dalton's chest and the other on Lina's shoulder. "I'll act as her bodyguard, since I understand you're on vacation and too closely involved in this matter in any case. I won't let anything happen to her." He offered his keys. "Take my vehicle and follow us, okay?"

If Lina's expression hadn't relaxed, Dalton might have said something vulgar. His wife was in good hands with his twin brother. He knew it.

"The two of you are something else," Dalton said in lieu of any curse words. He took Deke's car keys, sliding them into his front pocket.

To Lina he said, "Deke is a bodyguard. He won't let anything happen to you, I swear."

"I know," she said with a smile. "When I looked you up online at the library, I mostly found stuff about him. I figure I'm in the second best hands next to yours."

"Yes. Besides, I'll be following right behind them." He glanced down at the handcuffs. "Are those necessary?"

Miles nodded. "We need to put on a show for the others. Come on, Deke. Let's get out there."

To Lina, Miles said, "We're pretending to take this seriously to hopefully get your father to drop the charges. Are you ready to put on a show? If you could struggle, fight us the whole way to the vehicle and generally be averse to leaving with us, that would be helpful."

A sly smile surfaced on her face. "Don't worry. I have a bit of experience being difficult. I'm ready."

Dalton stopped them, kissed her rather passionately and then reluctantly released her into the hands of two men he'd give his life for, knowing they'd do the same for him and Lina if needed.

Outside the warehouse, he watched as Miles led a belligerent, swearing, difficult-to-manage Lina all the way to his vehicle.

"Where are you taking my daughter?" Ivan Dragovic roared as soon as she was brought outside.

Miles turned in his direction. "I'm executing the warrant for her arrest that you enabled. She'll be brought before the proper authorities in due time."

"No. The warrant isn't for her arrest. She was only supposed to be brought in for questioning," Martina Dragovic said. Her tone was pleading, but Dalton figured the underlying problem was the Dragovics didn't want to worry about Lina being charged and possibly losing the trust money she'd inherited from Mislav Zupan.

"Let us take her into our custody. That was what we intended all along."

"I don't care what you intended," Miles said. "That's not the way this works."

Ivan Dragovic said, "Do you know who I am?"

"Yes." A staring contest between the two ensued.

"Let her go into our custody. This is a private matter." Dragovic looked to his wife, who nodded.

She said, "Please let Nikolina come home with her family."

"No. That's not going to happen." Miles shrugged. "I don't care what was intended or that you miscalculated this being a private matter. What was written in the warrant has now been served lawfully and is the only consideration here."

Before the Dragovics could say anything else, Miles said, "If I were you, I'd be more worried about the charges they have on you for aiding and abetting a known criminal's passage into this country."

An FBI agent started reading the Dragovics a laundry list of offenses they might be charged with as they both demanded to speak to their lawyer. An ICE agent took Zupan and Kirill into custody. From across the space, Dalton saw Marko Zupan watch as his father and Kirill were arrested. He was free, so likely he'd also made a deal with local and federal law enforcement to get out from under *his* father's dictatorial thumb. If he'd worn a wire during the time he'd been in the warehouse, likely the feds had enough to hold them on a whole host of charges.

Kirill and Zupan gave each other dirty looks as they were handcuffed and loaded into another official vehicle.

Dalton found Deke's big SUV nearby and climbed inside to follow them to The Organization.

Once Dalton had parked Deke's vehicle in the ground floor parking garage at The Organization, he took the elevators to the fourth floor where the interrogation rooms were located.

The guy at reception took one look at him and pointed a thumb over his shoulder. "Room fifteen," he said as Dalton passed by him.

He called out a quick, "Thanks," over his shoulder and opened the door to room fifteen without knocking.

Deke waited with Lina. His brother smiled. "It took you long enough, bro. We've had quite a long discussion about you, haven't we, Lina?"

"Liar." Dalton eyed his wife, noticing her hands were free. "I saw the three of you standing close together by the elevator area when I parked. I'm amazed you had time to take her handcuffs off before I arrived up here."

"Oh, I took those off in the car."

"Where's Miles?"

"He went to expedite the paperwork to get Lina out of custody, tout the warrant as baseless, and get her freedom secured as soon as possible."

"Thanks, Deke."

"No worries."

"How is Chloe?"

Deke laughed. "Actually, she's pregnant."

"Really? I wondered about the car seats in the backseat of your SUV on my way over here."

"Those are for Reece's twins. Chloe has been helping with them, which is what I believe contributed to her current condition."

"I'd be willing to bet that you had more to do with her condition than Reece's kids did."

He laughed. "Maybe. And while she loves our niece and nephew, she wants a baby, too. So naturally, I was happy to help her out with that."

Dalton laughed and punched his brother in the arm. "Of course you were. I'm glad. Tell Chloe I said congrats."

Deke lifted one shoulder. "I'll tell her once she's not hovering over the toilet with cheeks the color of pale moonlight trying to keep meals down."

Miles opened the door and waltzed inside. "Okay, Lina. You're free to go. The charges have been dropped. When the judge got angry with your father for making up the information on the warrant, he said there had been a misunderstanding."

"Where are my parents? Do you know?"

"They were charged with helping Zupan, Kirill and Marko enter the country illegally, but I think those charges are about to be thrown out. Zupan and Kirill have had to be separated, as they seem to want to kill each other."

"Think it's true what Kirill said about being Zupan's son?" Dalton asked.

Miles shrugged. "I don't care, but either way they are both being deported back to Kzeratia under federal or international extradition orders, or possibly both.

"I suspect once at their final destination, they will be promptly chucked into a deep, dark hole for a long, long time regardless of whether they have a familial relationship or not. I say, good riddance.

"Meanwhile, the majority of the Zupan family assets in this country and Kzeratia have been frozen. Not sure about the Cayman Islands or Zurich accounts and I don't care either."

Dalton grabbed Lina's hand and asked, "What about the money they were after that Lina has control of? I have come to believe my wife might be a millionaire."

Miles shook his head. "Nope. She's a billionaire, but I'm afraid those funds are also frozen, for the time being at any rate. Guess you can't quit your day job after all, Dalton."

Dalton shrugged "Oh, well. Easy come, easy go."

Lina looked at him. "I only learned about the money today."

"Me, too," Dalton said.

"Is it really a billion dollars?" Lina asked.

Dalton smiled. "Actually two billion, four hundred million and some change."

Miles added, "But I wouldn't plan on inheriting any of it. The courts will be fighting about it for years to come, I suspect."

"Are you upset about losing that much money?"

"No. Are you?"

She laughed. "Not even a little bit. It's likely money from ill-gotten gains and shady deals. I never wanted any part of it."

"Good for you."

"And you're truly okay with me not having the money?"

"I don't care if you're a millionaire or penniless, Lina. I love you just the way you are." He leaned down to kiss her.

"You mean a food runner in Las Vegas living paycheck to paycheck in a crowded apartment with four other women?"

"Yes. I love her best. And I'm happy to support you in whatever you decide to do."

"I want to be with you. I don't care where we go or what job I get."

"Are you okay living in a more modest section of Ironwood?"

"Of course."

"And are you willing to travel with me when I go out of town?"

"Yes. I'll look forward to it."

Miles lifted his head and stared at them, frowning. "Wait a minute. The Organization doesn't exactly have a family plan for spouses to go out in the field with our operatives."

"Maybe you should develop one," Dalton said, never once taking his gaze from his wife's lovely face.

"Does she have any pertinent skills?"

"Oh she's very talented in many different ways."

Lina gave him a sexy, sultry-eyed stare. That look meant she wanted him. He smiled back. One corner of her mouth lifted in response.

Just like that first picture he'd seen of Lina in the bus station. Her pouty little mouth framed with lush, full lips barely quirked upward once again, sending his baser thoughts in a dangerously passionate direction.

"Somehow I don't think her skills would be beneficial to anyone but you," Miles said under his breath.

"We're free to go, right, Miles? I need to take my wife home and carry her over a threshold. It's tradition."

Lina smiled. "Tradition can be very important."

EPILOGUE

Key West, the biannual Langston gathering

"Are you sure your parents will like me?" Lina bounced back and forth on the balls of her feet as Dalton extracted their luggage from the taxi, wickedly nervous about meeting her in-laws.

He paid the driver and turned to her. "They will love you. How could they not? You're perfect."

"I'm the daughter of a well-known criminal threatened with indictment every other day, currently embroiled in charges that he aided and abetted another known criminal's entrance into this country for nefarious purposes involving me."

Her husband's brows narrowed. "Maybe we won't mention that right up front."

"And what about our unusual marriage?"

"What about it? We're married. The end."

"Do you think they'll be upset about the drive-through Vegas wedding, though? Will they be angry that the youngest—" Dalton's eyes widened with shock "—albeit the tallest, son didn't have a church wedding?"

Dalton laughed out loud. "No. Several of my brothers have eloped. Don't worry on that score."

"My family was less accepting of you."

"I have faith that they will come around. Especially if the account you inherited from your first husband becomes unfrozen."

"Do you think it will? I don't plan to take the money. The Zupans can have it back."

"Except that your parents *really* want that money. They will want you to fight to keep it."

"Maybe I'll give it all to my parents if they are willing to accept you—in writing. Or I'll tell them that you wanted it that way. Perhaps I can endear them to you through a generous monetary donation."

"If I could rate anything above a scurrilous look of hatred, it would be a miracle and I'd be delighted."

"Do you want to keep any of the money?"

"No. I make my own money."

"Good. I don't want it either." She grinned at him. "I also find great satisfaction in earning my money."

"Something else we have in common."

They'd discovered quite a few things they had in common over the past several days.

After Dalton took her to his home and carried her over the threshold there, he'd also made love to her for the better part of three days where they'd taken risk after risk, tempting fate over and over again. They'd slapped fate right across the chops repeatedly, but Lina hadn't gotten pregnant.

When he suggested taking a trip anywhere she wanted to go, she stopped taking chances temporarily and invested in a good birth control method. Then they made vacation plans. They left the next day for a weeklong road trip, traveling across the country, planning to end up in Key West for the latest Langston gathering.

She'd moved her meager belongings into Dalton's home. It wasn't a large house, but given her previous apartment arrangement with four other people in a two-bedroom place in Las Vegas, it seemed like a palace, with three bedrooms and two bathrooms, a dedicated office that wasn't one of the bedrooms and not only a living room but also a small, cozy den tucked away.

Lina was in love with Dalton and his house and his life. After his vacation, he was scheduled to go into a job undercover where he had to have a multitude of tattoos in order to fit into the situation he entered. His security firm was infiltrating a little known secretive gang of thugs and criminals on the outskirts of Las Vegas that had seemingly sprung up overnight.

The Organization, the private security company where Dalton and many of his brothers worked, had an amazing lab with lots of gadgets and techniques to make their operatives able to fit seamlessly into absolutely any situation.

Lina didn't mind tattoos, but the extensive nature of what was required for this coming undercover persona was quite a lot. Dalton didn't want to live with the tattoos forever, especially considering he'd also need a rather large rendering of the year *1983* in five-inch-tall numerals across his chest along with the Spanish translation of *my crazy life* in a different font across the year, which was a baseline requirement of the gang because it was the year their secretive leader had been born and apparently he had a crazy life.

She didn't blame him, as she'd seen a rendering of all the tattoos Dalton would have to put on his body. Lina had already requested a ringside seat to watch it done. Mostly she liked watching him without his shirt on.

She wished she could go along, but knew it was too dangerous. His brother Zak was going to be on this tattooed assignment with him. Lina and Zak's wife,

Kaitlin, already planned to hang out together for the duration of their time away from home.

Lina had met all of Dalton's brothers and most of their wives, but their parents had been on a trip overseas until this morning. She was still very nervous, although her sisters-in-law had helped allay her fears. They told her all about their plan to set him up on blind dates with various friends so he wouldn't be the only unmarried brother.

Kaitlin had divulged the family's previous plan to send Dalton on a string of blind dates if he didn't bring a plus one to the Key West gathering. She told Lina they were all glad Dalton had found someone he loved.

Lina expressed a brief doubt about whether his parents would be happy he'd married into the Dragovic family, but Kaitlin said she'd never seen Dalton so smitten.

"I was the first Langston wife in this boys' club. I've known Dalton for a few years now. He's *never* looked at any woman the way he looks at you. Trust me when I say, he's got it bad for you, Lina."

Dalton carried their luggage along the walkway along the side of the house to the back. He punched a number into a pad by the door. One loud click later and they entered a large kitchen.

"Dalton? Is that you?" a woman's voice asked from deeper inside the house. An older woman who had the same color eyes as Dalton came into the room.

"Hi, Mom," Dalton dropped their bags near the back door and hugged her.

"I'd like you to meet Lina…" he paused and turned toward her, "my wife."

His mother winked and looked over her shoulder at Lina. She leaned in and mock-whispered, "I'm supposed to pretend to throw a fit that my youngest boy and last unmarried child has eloped and that I'm unhappy about it." She rolled her eyes, leaned in and hugged Lina. "But I'm not the least bit upset. Besides, it's not in my nature to be angry with anyone. Welcome to the family, honey."

The door into the kitchen opened suddenly and Veronica, dressed in a slinky bikini, strolled in, walked straight up to Dalton and threw her arms around his neck, kissing his cheek, but also clinging to him like white on rice.

"Veronica?" he said, hoping Lina wouldn't think he'd lied about their relationship.

"I'm so glad you're here, Dalton. The place just isn't the same without you." She nuzzled his neck and he stiffened, refusing to hug her back or respond in any way.

Next to him, Lina said, "I thought you said Veronica didn't like you in that way. You said she loved Alex."

Veronica kissed him on the cheek again. "That's true, but it's so much fun to torture any of the brothers." She laughed and broke her fierce hold on him. "Good heavens, he's so stiff I'm afraid if I hug him any longer he'll snap in half."

Lina laughed too. Veronica immediately hugged Lina like they were long-lost sisters separated at birth. "You're right," Lina said, still laughing. "That was so much fun."

Dalton looked at his wife. "You set that up?"

"Yes." Lina grinned at him, still linked arm in arm with Veronica.

"I didn't think the two of you had met."

"Not in person, until now. But we spoke on the phone. Veronica is cool. I'm not jealous of her anymore."

"The truth is, I'm jealous of *her*. And I can't wait until your parents find out you married the daughter of a mobster." Veronica's eyes widened all the way after spilling the news.

"Lina is the daughter of a mobster?" Dalton's mother said with a questioning look.

"My full name is Nikolina Dragovic Langston."

Even his mother knew who Ivan Dragovic was, but instead of being worried or upset, she smiled and said, "Ooh, a mob princess? Isn't that exciting! I'll bet you have lots of interesting stories."

Several male voices rose in another room.

Dalton said, "I'm going to go in and tell them all that you were so upset by mom's fit of temper, Veronica's flirtation and the knowledge that you're originally a Dragovic being revealed unexpectedly that you ran out and left me."

Lina laughed again, hugging Veronica and his mother to each of her sides like they were already best friends. "This family is so much fun. I can't wait to find out what happens next."

THE END

AVAILABLE NOW

BIKER
BAD BOYS IN BIG TROUBLE 1

Despite the danger, there are some definite pluses to undercover agent Zak Langston's current alias as a mechanic slash low-life criminal. He doesn't have to shave regularly or keep his hair military short. He gets to ride a damn fine Harley. And then there's the sweet, sexy lady next door who likes to sneak peeks at his butt. Yeah, that was a major plus.

Kaitlin Price has had the worst luck with men. As if her unearned reputation as a frigid tease isn't enough, she also has to deal with her stepsister's casual cruelty and taunting tales of sexual conquests she can only dream of. So Kaitlin has never been with a man. So what? So what…

So maybe the sexy bad boy next door would be willing to help her with that.

Gunfire, gangsters and a kidnapping weren't part of her Deflower Kaitlin plan. Good thing for her bad boy Zak is very, very good. At everything.

BOUNCER
BAD BOYS IN BIG TROUBLE 2

DEA Agent Reece Langston has spent a year at the city's hottest club, working his way closer to the core of a money laundering operation. Women throw themselves at him all the time, but there's only one he's interested in catching. And she won't even tell him her name.

FBI Agent Jessica Hayes doesn't know much about the sexy stranger except that he's tall, dark and gorgeous. Best of all, he seems just as drawn to her as she is to him—in other words, he's the perfect man to show one kick-ass virgin what sex is all about. No names, no strings and no regrets.

Their one-night stand turns into two. Then a date. Then…maybe more.

Everything is going deliciously well until Jessica's boss orders her to use her lover to further an FBI operation.

Everything is going deliciously well until Reece's handler orders him to use his lover to get closer to his target.

Is their desire enough to match the danger and deception?

BODYGUARD
BAD BOYS IN BIG TROUBLE 3

The baseball stadium is torture for Chloe Wakefield, from the noisy stands to the slimy man her colleague set her up with. Too bad she isn't with the sexy stud seated on her other side. He shares his popcorn. Shields her from the crowd. And, when the kiss cam swings their way, gives her a lip-lock that knocks her socks into the next county.

Goodbye, vile blind date. Hello, gorgeous stranger.
Staying under the radar is pretty much a job requisite for bodyguard Deke Langston, but he can't resist tasting Chloe's sweet lips. Nor her sweet invitation into her bed, where the sensuous little virgin proceeds to blow his mind.

But someone doesn't like how close they are getting. The thought that scares Deke the most is that another woman in his care might be hurt because of his past.

All of Deke's skills are put to the test as he and Chloe race to solve the puzzle of who is plotting against them.

Chloe's in danger and Deke has never had a more precious body to guard.

BOMB TECH
BAD BOYS IN BIG TROUBLE 4

Bomb tech and firefighter Alex Langston has a reputation around the station as a bad-boy, love 'em and leave 'em type, but that couldn't be further from the truth. He wants nothing more than a quiet life after a military tour that saw him in some very hot situations overseas. He garners more than his fair share of feminine attention, but hasn't felt so much as a spark of interest for any woman since landing in Ironwood, Arizona…until now.

Schoolteacher Veronica Quentin was warned to keep her guard up around Alex. The last thing she wants is to be a notch on some sexy stud's bedpost. She's been used before, and knows well the heartache that can bring. But that was before she saw him. And before he rescued her from a mysterious kidnapping that saw her chained half-naked in the town square with a bomb strapped to her chest.

But is Veronica the real target? Or has someone set their sights on Alex?

Until they find out, they can't trust anyone but each other. And the sensual flames that ignite whenever they're together.

BANDIT
BAD BOYS IN BIG TROUBLE 6

Miles Turner, a handler and operative with The Organization, a private security firm, is used to always being the man with the plan, the guy in control of everything around him. He can't imagine any situation that would get the better of him—until he meets Sophie.

Travelling sales rep Sophie Rayburn has been burned by love before, but she's determined not to spend Christmas Eve alone. When she spots sexy Miles at a run-down bar in a Podunk New Mexico bar, she decides he'd make the perfect gift to herself. Why shouldn't she indulge them both with a little holiday cheer between the sheets?

Sensual sparks fly as soon as they come together, like they were made for each other, in bed and out. A kidnapping, a drug scam and a dangerous mole don't stand a chance.

Sweet, sexy Sophie is enough to make even a good man lose total control. And Miles is not good. He's all bad boy.

CLOSE ENCOUNTERS OF THE ALIEN KIND
NOCTURNE FALLS UNIVERSE

Pilot. Guard. Prisoner.

All three are crashed in the Georgia woods, lost on a world where extraterrestrials are the stuff of science fiction. Blending into the human world is doable, if dangerous. But what if the locals are far from human themselves, with secrets of their own?

Former bounty hunter Stella Grey grew up an orphan on family-centric Alpha-Prime, so she knows the value of belonging. Leaving everything—and everyone—behind to join distant kin a galaxy away in Alienn, Arkansas, is a small price to pay.

Heading up a retrieval operation following a spacecraft crash in rural Georgia is her chance to prove herself to them. Her mission? Locate the ship's occupants. Secure the prisoner. And, above all, keep the earthlings from discovering that aliens live and walk among them.

Draeken Phoenix is the bad boy from one of Alpha-Prime's best families, known for getting in and out of scrapes with wit, charm and sheer bravado. He never expected to become an actual prisoner bound for a galactic gulag. Until now, the worst thing that had ever happened to him was losing the woman he loved. But he has a plan.

He's bet his life on it.

COMING SOON

YOU'VE GOT ALIENS

First in the Alienn, Arkansas series

About the Author

FIONA ROARKE is a multi-published author who lives a quiet life with the exception of the characters and stories roaming around in her head. She writes about sexy alpha heroes and used them to launch her very first series, *Bad Boys in Big Trouble*.

Next up, a new Sci-Fi contemporary romance series set in Arkansas. When she's not curled on the sofa reading a great book or at the movie theater watching the latest action film, Fiona spends her time writing about the next bad boy (or bad boy alien) who needs his story told.

A hearty dose of laughter, each and every day, is required along with lots of coffee first thing in the morning as important parts of her routine.

FIND FIONA ONLINE:
www.FionaRoarke.com
www.facebook.com/FionaRoarke
https://twitter.com/fiona_roarke

Want to know when Fiona's next book will be available? Sign up for her Newsletter: http://eepurl.com/bONukX

Printed in Great Britain
by Amazon

86169996R00139